"Are you warning me off?" Georgina asked

Janus moved closer. "Only because I am certain marriage to Miles would be a disaster for you," he replied.

"Look, Mr. Stanhope," she said impatiently. "It's my opinion that Miles should be able to marry or cohabit with anyone he chooses. He's twenty-five years old."

"I still think you should give him up." Janus suddenly seized her hand. "Is there no way I can persuade you?"

Georgina quivered at his touch. Oh, yes, she thought, there were a hundred ways, and she'd probably enjoy every one. But he still had no right to warn her—or anyone else—against marrying his little brother.

She removed her hand sharply. "No, Mr. Stanhope. I'm not open to persuasion."

His glittering dark eyes held admiration. "In that case, Miss Georgina Griffiths, our paths must inevitably cross again."

Catherine George was born in Wales, and following her marriage to an engineer, lived in Brazil for eight years at a gold-mine site. It was an experience she would later draw upon for her books, when she and her husband returned to England. Now her husband helps manage their household so that Catherine can devote more time to her writing. They have two children—a daughter and a son—who share their mother's love of language and writing.

Books by Catherine George

HARLEQUIN ROMANCE

2822—THE FOLLY OF LOVING
2924—MAN OF IRON
2942—THIS TIME ROUND
3081—CONSOLATION PRIZE
3129—ARROGANT INTERLOPER
3147—A CIVILISED ARRANGEMENT

HARLEQUIN PRESENTS

1016—LOVE LIES SLEEPING
1065—TOUCH ME IN THE MORNING
1152—VILLAIN OF THE PIECE
1184—TRUE PARADISE
1225—LOVEKNOT
1255—EVER SINCE EDEN
1321—COME BACK TO ME

UNLIKELY CUPID
Catherine George

Harlequin Books

TORONTO • NEW YORK • LONDON
AMSTERDAM • PARIS • SYDNEY • HAMBURG
STOCKHOLM • ATHENS • TOKYO • MILAN

Original hardcover edition published in 1991
by Mills & Boon Limited

ISBN 0-373-03177-7

Harlequin Romance first edition February 1992

UNLIKELY CUPID

CHAPTER ONE

THE joyous urgency of wedding bells hurried Georgina along as she reached the outskirts of Keyne Magna. She made straight for the village green as instructed, parked her car in the shade of a cedar tree alongside the Old Forge Garage, then reached over into the back seat for her hat. With the aid of the driving mirror she made sure every last strand of hair was tucked away under the swathe of silk which formed the turban-like crown, adjusted the wide straw brim so that it tilted low over her eyes, then drew on her gloves, picked up her small suede bag and slid reluctantly from the car to join the stream of wedding guests passing through the lych-gate of the church across the green. The women ahead of her were for the most part arrayed in fluttering, fragile dresses and large, extravagant hats, the men in black morning suits with top hats at jaunty angles, but no one, Georgina noted with gloom, was arriving alone.

Suffering badly from stagefright, Georgina walked on leaden feet past ancient, leaning tombstones. She dawdled, lagging behind the others, until she could postpone the evil moment no longer. The tall usher standing alone in the church porch had spotted her. He greeted Georgina with a polite, welcoming smile which altered to a look of startled enquiry as his eyes met hers. He frowned, head on one side, his eyes narrowed under close-cut dark hair as curly as her own. The face beneath it was tanned and narrow, with a scar on one cheekbone, a slight dent at the bridge of his nose and a wide, well-cut mouth above a cleft chin. And having looked at the face just once Georgina felt as though the stone flags of the church porch were shifting beneath her expensive new shoes.

She pulled herself together sharply, aware that this quite wonderful man was saying something for the second time. And smiling that devastating smile again. The smile which haunted her dreams.

'These bells are deafening,' he said. 'Did you say ''bride'' or ''groom''?'

Barbs of guilt pierced Georgina. In actual fact she was friend of neither. 'Oh—bride,' she said, in a voice so breathless her own mother would never have recognised it.

'Have we met?' he asked, moving closer.

She shook her head. 'No.' Which they hadn't exactly. But she'd seen him before. Just once.

They were interrupted by a thin young man in formal wedding garb who shot from the church to grab Georgina by the hand. 'Gee, darling, you made it—well done!' He grinned up at the man beside him. 'Trust you to steal a march on me, Janus. Hang on here, would you, while I take Georgina inside, then I'll come back to wait with you for Katie?'

Escorted by Miles Stanhope, the man to blame for her presence at the wedding, Georgina walked down the aisle of the church, glad of her concealing hat brim as she was shown to a pew not far behind those occupied by the bride's family. Miles whispered something in her ear, then took himself off, leaving Georgina to slide to her knees for a few moments on an embroidered hassock before sitting to await the arrival of the bride, utterly shattered by the fact that the man she'd been dreaming about for the past couple of weeks was actually Janus Stanhope, not only brother of Miles, but the type of man who, if he'd lived in a former era, would have been described as a libertine, or rake, or philanderer, or any term which described his danger to those members of the opposite sex who caught his eye.

The bride was late. Georgina, doing her best to be inconspicuous, gazed down steadfastly at her gloved hands, bitterly regretting that she'd let Miles plead and wheedle and cajole her into coming, much against her will, to the wedding of a girl she'd never met in her life. If she'd known she was to discover that the man she'd once glimpsed for a moment at the Chelsea Flower Show was Janus Stanhope, and not St George and Sir Galahad rolled into one, nothing on earth would have persuaded her to come. Miles, she thought acidly, had a lot to answer for.

Georgina was not, as she was the first to admit, a morning person. The telephone had rung for ages early that fateful Sunday before it roused her from sleep. She'd reached out a groping hand for the receiver, her eyes still glued shut as she muttered a hoarse hello.

'Gee, darling, I'm a bit of a fix,' said a coaxing male voice.

Georgina shuddered. 'Go away.' She put the phone down, dragging the covers over her head to recapture blissful oblivion, but the telephone rang again immediately. With a frustrated sigh she gave in and sat up, pushing her hair out of her eyes as she snatched the receiver off the hook.

'Whatever it is—*no!*' she said balefully.

'How did you know it was me?' demanded Miles Stanhope.

'Who else would ring me at this hour on a Sunday morning! I was enjoying my only lie-in of the week, you sadist.'

'But I must see you, Gee! I need your help.'

'No fear—I still carry the scars from last time. Get my big brother to bale you out—he's your mate, not me.'

'Afraid Harry won't do.'

'Why not?'

'A matter of gender, old love. I need a woman.'

'What?' Georgina glared at the receiver, incensed.

'Not in that way,' said Miles hastily. 'I mean I want you to come to a wedding.'

'You're getting married?' she asked, brightening.

'Absolutely not!' Miles sounded horrified at the very idea. 'Look, Gee, it's nothing sinister, I swear. If you let me take you out to lunch I'll explain.'

'Where are you then?'

'In the usual place. But I can drive down right away.'

'Important enough to bring you chasing down here from London, no less! Oh, all right. But I'm only saying yes to lunch, Miles. I'm promising nothing. And don't you dare turn up here before half-twelve at the earliest.'

What a fool she'd been to say yes, even to lunch, thought Georgina bitterly as she listened to strains

of Handel on the organ. Previous experience of
Miles should have taught her better. But when he'd
turned up at her flat that Sunday he'd looked so
harassed and woebegone she'd softened towards
him enough to listen.

'Thing is,' he'd informed her with a sigh, 'I've
got three problems. First, I've got a girlfriend.'

'So what's new?'

Hunted blue eyes pleaded with Georgina's. 'I
know, I know, but my grandmother's got a bit of
a bee in the proverbial bonnet about this one.'

'You're a big boy, Miles. Old enough to have
girlfriends, I'd have thought.'

Miles, as Georgina knew from Harry, was something of a disappointment to his family. Instead of
following in the family banking tradition he was
determined to make a living as a photographer. His
manner was defensive as he produced a photograph from his pocket. 'Linda's a model. I took
her out for a picnic and persuaded her to pose for
me. This was the result—I sold it to one of the
tabloids.'

Georgina was much impressed by the photograph. Taken in full sun on a stretch of sandy
beach, the girl stood poised on tiptoe for flight,
naked except for a minuscule white towel draped
around her hips, her tangled mane of curls ob-
scuring her face but leaving her spectacular breasts
bare. Georgina's praise failed to lift Miles's gloom.
He was, he informed her despondently, commanded to take his lady love to his sister's wedding.

Georgina, amused, advised him to tell his little
friend to wear a few more clothes, but otherwise
could see no problem.

Miles looked uncomfortable. 'It's not just that,' he muttered. 'I mean—well, how can I put it? Linda's got a face and body the camera dotes on, but the voice doesn't match, and she's not exactly brimming with the old grey matter, either.'

Georgina, disgusted, accused him of snobbery.

Miles looked injured. 'Qualms I may have had, Gee, but I asked her, honestly, exactly as bidden. Linda just laughed in my face. She doesn't want to come to the wedding. Not her scene, she said.' His expressive face grew bleak. 'I'm not the only pebble on her cute little beach by a long way, Georgina.'

'Ah!'

'Thing is, Gee, my grandmother's a fair age, and her ticker's a bit fragile. Dad's quite worried about her. He says if I upset her about my girlfriend it might bring on a heart attack, which at the very least would spoil Katie's wedding. Besides, we all love the old tartar. I don't *want* to upset her, even though she ordered me to bring my young woman to the wedding, or else.' Miles looked harassed. 'Not sure what she means by ''or else''—probably means to cut me out of her will.'

By that stage Georgina realised what he had in mind, and refused point-blank to take on the role of his 'young woman' for the day, in place of the ineligible Linda. Miles was quick to assure her she'd be introduced to his family as herself, not the model they'd heard about, but even so it cost him the most expensive lunch the Unicorn could provide and four hours of solid argument before he finally bludgeoned Georgina, totally against her better judgement, into giving in. He even offered to foot the bill for her outfit. This last, if nothing else, convinced Georgina how deadly serious he was about the whole thing, though his third problem, which concerned one Miss Rosalind Winter, Georgina couldn't see in the light of a problem at all.

Young Ros, Miles said unhappily, was his sister Katie's best friend, and had been after him since she was ten years old. Now he was to be usher and Ros bridesmaid he was scared to death.

'What a wimp you are, Miles!' Georgina told him scornfully.

'I admit it! But for pity's sake say you'll be my lady for the day, Gee,' he'd pleaded. 'One way and another I'm in sore need of protection.'

In the end Georgina, deeply reluctant, had capitulated. Which, she thought grimly, was why she was here now in this lovely little church, under much scrutiny from various Stanhopes, and pretending, heaven help her, to be Miles's fiancée. This last touch, he'd declared, had been vital to convince Rosalind she was on a losing wicket. How she wished Harry were here, thought Georgina, as she cast a professional eye over the flower arrangements. But Harry was, at this very moment, the lucky devil, baking himself black on a sunny Greek beach, instead of lending his little sister much-needed moral support.

A surreptitious look at the other guests provided some consolation. Georgina decided she looked at least as good as most of the women, possibly better than some. The silk of her severe little suit was the same shade as the natural straw of her extravagantly large hat, both items far more expensive than her usual clothes. Not that Miles had been allowed to pay for any of it. Georgina had insisted on buying her own suit, and the hat was on loan from her mother, destined for another wedding later on in the summer. Like her mother, Georgina was tall and generously curved, but there the resemblance ended. Margaret Griffiths and her son Harry were dark of hair and eye, whereas Georgina's hair was red and curly like her father's, her eyes any shade from steel-grey to translucent green according to mood, and, to her everlasting despair, she was blessed with freckles which lent her the appealing, presentable air Miles seemed to think ideal to impress his family with his taste in girlfriends.

At long last the bells stopped, a ripple ran through the congregation, and the organist began the sedate, familiar chords which heralded the entry of the bride. All heads turned as Katherine Stanhope, blonde and radiant in satin and pearls, began the walk down the aisle on her father's arm, followed first by a thin dark girl in pink, then by a coterie of little white-clad girls and boys whose progress, hand in hand, brought tears to feminine eyes already dewy at the first glimpse of the bride.

Miles slid in beside Georgina with a sigh of relief. 'Just pray this lot behaves,' he whispered, scowling ferociously at a small boy on the point of breaking formation. 'Move over, Gee.'

Georgina stared fixedly in front of her as Janus Stanhope slid into the seat alongside Miles. But a stronger will than hers compelled her to turn her head slightly at last, whereupon her gaze locked with a narrowed dark one for a disgracefully long interval before Miles gave her a nudge, and she jumped guiltily to her feet for the first hymn.

Georgina knew the words of 'Love Divine, All Loves Excelling' well enough, but her voice refused point-blank to function. She mouthed the words, staring at the wedding programme in her gloved hands, conscious of Miles singing lustily off-key beside her, while beyond him the deeper tones of another voice struck an answering chord inside her which had nothing at all to do with music. There was no mistake. Janus Stanhope was quite definitely the man she'd met so fleetingly in Chelsea.

Like an automaton Georgina sat when the others sat, bowed her head in prayer at the requisite points, listened to the bridal couple making their responses, while all the time, without a single further glance in his direction, she remained as conscious of Janus Stanhope's physical presence as though he were actually beside her instead of Miles. Georgina glanced down at her front, astonished to find it remarkably stationary despite the gymnastics her heart was performing under the silk. Could it really happen like this? Even after discovering that the man of her dreams was an accomplished rake, she seemed to have suffered the renowned *coup de foudre* just the same. She'd read about the thunderclap of falling in love, of course, but had dismissed it as romantic poppycock. Until her first look at Janus Stanhope a couple of weeks ago. Even then she'd dismissed her feelings as a figment of her imagination. But it was no imagination right now. He sat only a foot or so from her in the flesh, and the shock waves buffeting her were all too physical a fact. Her brain could tell her how silly she was as much as it liked. Her heart and body were taking no notice at all, both of them experi-

encing a response to Janus Stanhope which made
it difficult for their owner to sit still in her pew.

Georgina sat straighter, staring rigidly ahead of
her as Miles muttered something in her ear then left
with his brother to join the wedding party in the
vestry. But her eyes developed a will of their own,
trained on the tall figure of Janus Stanhope every
step of the way as he followed his younger brother
up the aisle in the wake of the others. Then something occurred to Georgina. All this romantic
languishing, she reminded herself acidly, was a bit
silly anyway, since the object of it all was under the
mistaken impression that she belonged to his
brother.

It was a salutary thought. Georgina's faculties
began functioning normally again. As the bride
began her triumphal progress down the aisle on the
arm of her bridegroom Georgina stood up with the
rest, in reasonable command of herself now as she
watched the procession wend its way to the church
door. Miles made urgent gestures at her as he
passed, plainly suspicious she might cut and run
now the service was over, and Georgina smiled back
at him reassuringly, this time keeping her eyes firmly
averted from the tall figure pacing indolently at
Miles's side.

To an accompaniment of Bach organ music the
majority of the guests were shepherded outside by
a side door while the wedding group subjected
themselves to photographs in the church porch.
Miles hurried to Georgina when she finally emerged
a long way behind the others. She felt shy, she found
to her dismay, and smiled more warmly at him than
usual as he took her arm.

'Thanks for coming, Gee,' he said gratefully and ran his eyes over her, obviously seeing her properly for the first time. 'I say, you do look stunning, old love. What a fantastic hat!'

'The biggest I could find to hide under!'

He laughed. 'Look, I must take a few shots of Katie and Angus, if only to show my family what a clever lad I am with the old Box Brownie. They wouldn't trust me with the whole show. I'll only be a few minutes then we can walk next door to the reception and I'll introduce you to everyone.'

Georgina felt like St Sebastian as curious glances came at her like arrows from all directions. 'Miles,' she said apprehensively, 'I've got the most awful cold feet about all this.'

'Nonsense.' He gave her an affectionate pat on the cheek, then dashed off with his camera, eager to outdo the professional photographer at his job.

Georgina retreated to a group of sheltering ilex to watch the wedding group from a distance, as Miles, stentorian with his instructions, first posed the bride and groom, then a family group, yelling at the children in their frills and knee-breeches as he brought them under control with the aid of a girl who had to be the Rosalind he was trying to elude. Georgina eyed the girl in pink with curiosity. She'd pictured someone bosomy and giggly, with well-bred equine features, but Rosalind was pin-thin and darkly pretty, also efficient and unfailingly good-humoured as she disciplined her little charges to stand still long enough to have their photographs taken for the umpteenth time.

At last Georgina gave up struggling to keep her eyes away from Janus Stanhope. It was hopeless anyway. He drew her like a magnet. Although no taller or larger than many of the other men, to Georgina he stood out from the rest. There was something about the way he held himself, she thought dreamily, a look of assurance and authority and—and grace. All of which, Georgina informed herself scathingly, was in the eye of one bird-brained beholder. She wrenched her eyes away and began to read the inscriptions on the nearest tombstones, thinking how strange it was that he resembled Miles so little. If she'd ever given any thought to Janus Stanhope at all, except as the boring subject of Mile's incessant outpourings, she'd pictured him as fair and blue-eyed, with the ineluctably Anglo-Saxon look of his sibling.

'Isn't it time we introduced ourselves properly?' said a voice behind her. Georgina's heart thumped under the tailored silk of her jacket as she turned slowly to face the man monopolising her thoughts.

Seen again at close quarters, Janus Stanhope was less regularly handsome than from a distance. His teeth were very white, but just slightly crooked, and one side of his wide mouth lifted higher than the other, as if reaching towards the scar on his cheekbone. His face was longer and bonier than Miles's, he was half a head taller and several pounds heavier, and all in all quite the most attractive man Georgina had laid eyes on in her entire life.

'I'm Janus Stanhope,' he said as Georgina regarded him in silence from the shelter of her hat brim.

'How do you do,' she replied, putting out a hand to take the slim, hard one offered her. 'Georgina Griffiths.'

The touch of Janus Stanhope's fingers reacted on her like an electric shock, right through the doeskin of her mother's best gloves. Georgina took an iron grip on herself. If she didn't get herself together pretty quickly the man would think she was an idiot!

'It was good of you to spare the time from your work to come today,' went on Janus, smiling at her with such easy familiarity that she was struck by a sudden, seductive thought. Had he by any strange chance experienced the same chemistry? Quite an ego-boost if such a celebrated heartbreaker took a fancy to a simple country maiden like me, she thought with satisfaction.

Encouraged by the thought, Georgina's smile widened, her eyes glittering beneath the flattering brim. 'My mother offered herself as substitute if things get hectic while I'm away.'

He looked startled. 'Your mother? Does she do the same sort of thing?'

'Not very often.' Georgina shrugged a little. 'My father doesn't like it much, so it's strictly emergency procedure.'

The slim black brows met above the rather attractive dent at the bridge of Janus Stanhope's nose. 'But he doesn't object to *your* work?'

'Oh, no. He's all for it. He lent me the money to get started, in fact.'

'Pretty sporting of him.' Janus's smile altered subtly, grew more intimate. He moved closer, then his eyes lit with a sudden flash of pure annoyance as Miles, beaming happily, dashed up to interrupt them.

'There you are, you two. Introduced yourselves?'

'Of course.' Janus eyed him quizzically. 'Have *you* finished shooting everyone in sight?'

'Certainly have.' Miles seized Georgina by the elbow. 'We're to follow on to the house after the others. Gran's demanding your presence, Janus. Insists she can't totter that far without your arm to lean on.'

Janus excused himself gracefully to Georgina, a look in his eye she interpreted as a promise to spend more time with her later. She watched him go with regret, coming to with a start as Miles asked for what was obviously the second time what she thought of his legendary brother.

'He seems nice.' Nice! Hardly the adjective to apply to a man with Janus Stanhope's reputation! Georgina gave Miles a wry little smile as she gestured in the direction of Rosalind, who was marshalling her troupe of little darlings for the short walk from the church to the Stanhope home on the other side of the high stone wall. '*She* seems nice, too,' she said with meaning.

'Oh, Ros is OK,' said Miles carelessly as they strolled in the wake of the wedding party. 'Just not my type, that's all.'

'She's quite splendid with those children.'

'Plenty of practice—kindergarten teacher.'

'She doesn't look dangerous in the least, Miles. Certainly not enough for you to want me along as your minder!'

'You don't know her as I do.' He led her out of the churchyard and in through the gates in the walls which surrounded Glebe House. The house adjoined the church, but Georgina was given no time for appreciation of seventeenth-century architecture, much as she would have liked to look and linger. Miles whisked her along the stone-flagged paths leading round the house to the lawns which lay behind it, and, more importantly, to the striped awning along the walkway to the large marquee where the bridal party were still lined up, waiting to welcome the late arrivals.

'Come *on*, Miles,' called the bride. 'Angus is dying of thirst.'

'When isn't he?' Miles grinned, clapping his new brother-in-law on the shoulder before kissing his jubilant, pretty sister. 'This is Georgina.'

Georgina proffered her best wishes to the bride, who gave her a friendly, curious smile before introducing her euphoric young groom, who looked as though the worries of the world had rolled off his shoulders now the wedding ceremony was over. Miles took Georgina along the row of expectant relatives, rather like the English cricket captain introducing the Queen to his team at Lord's, and she shook hands and said the customary things to the bridegroom's parents, then braced herself to greet a formidable lady dressed in the style made popular by the Queen Mother. A pair of dark, bright eyes very like Janus Stanhope's examined Georgina with a searching scrutiny from beneath the upturned brim of a plumed straw hat.

'This,' said Miles, squeezing Georgina's hand encouragingly, 'is my grandmother.'

'I'm so pleased you could come, Miss Griffiths,' said Mrs Stanhope cordially. 'We've all been looking forward to meeting you.'

Georgina felt racked with guilt. 'It was kind of you to invite me.' She smiled valiantly, then held out her hand to Oliver Stanhope, the bride's father, who greeted her with a gleam in his eye very like that of his elder son.

'Delighted!' he said, taking her by the hand and, to Georgina's utter dismay, actually giving her a kiss on the cheek. 'I didn't credit Miles with such taste.'

'Oliver!' his mother said irately. 'What must the poor girl think of us?' She cast a comprehensive look about the marquee. 'See that Miss Griffiths has something to drink. It's almost time to take our places at table.'

'I'll take care of that,' said Janus smoothly, and with practised skill annexed Georgina from under Miles's nose to escort her across the polished board floor of the marquee, threading his way through the guests gathered in convivial groups. He beckoned to a hovering waiter and took two glasses from his tray.

'Don't be afraid of my grandmother,' Janus said softly, bending slightly to smile at her under the hat brim. 'Her bark's worse than her bite.'

Georgina was relieved to hear it. 'I'm not *afraid* of her exactly.'

'Nevertheless it must be a bit of an ordeal, having to meet us all *en masse* like this.'

She smiled at him wryly. 'The prospect was a little daunting.'

Janus eyed her over his glass. 'You're not at all what I expected, you know.'

Georgina would have given much to ask what he meant, but at that moment the red-coated toast-master took up position on a podium in the middle of the polished floor and began calling out the order of seating at the various tables.

Georgina found, to her mingled joy and apprehension, that she was to sit next to Janus, with Miles opposite, among a group of cousins and friends near the top table set apart for the bridal party. Miles, in his usual cavalier fashion, became engrossed instantly in the latest doings of his cousins, leaving Janus to perform the necessary introductions. For more than one reason it was hard for Georgina to relax enough to enjoy the meal itself much. Her physical proximity to Janus Stanhope proved to be a very effective appetite depressant, she found, particularly when coupled with the guilt she felt every time she looked up to find Rosalind Winter's dark eyes trained on her. The chief bridesmaid, who by this time had surrendered her charges into their parents' care, was sitting next to the best man and doing her utmost to look happy about it.

Georgina, irritated with Miles in one way for leaving her so much to her own devices, couldn't help feeling grateful to him otherwise, since Janus very plainly felt it necessary to pay his brother's guest all the attention Miles was bestowing elsewhere.

'I apologise for Miles—he doesn't see much of the family normally,' said Janus, as the first course was removed.

Georgina assured him she didn't mind in the least. Which was the simple truth. If Janus felt obliged to make up for his brother's neglect she was quite happy for Miles to ignore her completely all afternoon. Admittedly Miles beamed across at her

now and then with a casual, 'All right, Gee?' But
since he took her response for granted and immediately plunged back into his game of 'do you
remember?' with his pretty cousins, a wry smile
curved Georgina's mouth as she nodded in
response.

'Are you?' asked Janus in her ear. 'All right, I
mean? Or shall I bring Miles to heel for you?'

Georgina turned her eyes on him, their irises
green as bottleglass in the shadow of her hat brim.
'Yes, to the first, and, no, to the second.'

'Even though Miles is neglecting you? Which,'
he added in an undertone, 'I must be honest and
say is all to the good from my own personal point
of view.'

Georgina's eyes fell from the look in his, her heart
thumping, hardly knowing what she ate. Her entire
attention seemed suddenly taken up by the fact that
Janus Stanhope's black sleeve was brushing her pale
silk one, his foot occasionally making contact with
hers beneath the table, his hand beneath her elbow
as they rose to make the toasts. At last the speeches
were over and the bride and groom began threading
their way, smiling and laughing, through the tables,
on their way into the house to change for their
honeymoon journey.

Miles signalled wildly for Georgina's attention.
'Gran wants us. Come on, Gee. Better get it over
with. She's determined to have a chat with you.'

Janus rose as Georgina, jittery with nerves, got
to her feet. 'She won't eat you,' he murmured in
her ear, and she flashed him a grateful smile.

'Do come *on*, Gee,' said Miles, looking daggers
at his brother.

'A little late in the day for the proprietorial act,' said Georgina acidly, as Miles took her by the arm to circle the top table.

'What do you mean?'

'I mean, Miles Stanhope, that if your idea was to convince people I'm your property you've had a pretty queer way of showing it the last hour or two!'

'Oh, sorry. But I haven't seen Babs and Polly and the others for ages.' Miles gave her an odd look. 'Anyway, you weren't neglected, were you? Janus seemed quite happy to keep you entertained.'

Georgina gave him a fulminating look. 'That's not the point, is it?' She was prevented from giving him a larger piece of her mind by the fact that Henrietta Stanhope was beckoning her to sit beside her. With a feeling of doom Georgina sat down obediently, subjecting herself meekly to an intent scrutiny from the shrewd old eyes, while Miles joined the best man and Rosalind, an arrangement greeted by the latter with unconcealed delight.

'So,' said Henrietta Stanhope. 'You're the girl Miles is chasing after. Interesting. Somehow or other I'd never imagined freckles. Have you tried cucumber milk on them, child?'

Georgina returned the scrutiny steadily. 'Indeed I have, Mrs Stanhope. I've tried cucumber, sour milk and every mortal thing under the sun, short of household bleach, but the freckles soldier on, undefeated.'

The handsome, formidable face relaxed, and Mrs Stanhope laughed. 'Not only freckles, but spirit, too. Good. I like that. Tell me something about yourself.'

Georgina did her best, giving a brief résumé of her job in the small market town near the River Severn, the club where she played squash and badminton in the evenings, the family home in Hereford where she spent most Sundays. It was hot by this time in the marquee and Georgina's face, as she knew only too well, was milk-pale with mingled heat and tension, her freckles well in evidence by the time Miles saw fit to rescue her.

'You're an absolute brick,' he said in her ear after they'd taken their leave of Mrs Stanhope. He beamed at her, his eyes brilliant with gratitude. 'You've made a terrific hit with my grandmother. Janus is impressed, too, you know, which is rare. He doesn't go much for my girlfriends as a rule.'

'I'm not your girlfriend,' Georgina reminded him sharply.

'Shut up, love, for Pete's sake.' Miles cast a hunted look about him to see who was within earshot, but everyone was milling around in groups as guests left their places to talk with others. The only eyes turned in her direction, Georgina saw with a leap of her pulse, belonged to Janus, and as though he were responding to her unspoken plea he rose from his place among his cousins and came to her side.

'You survived the audience with my grandmother?' he asked, his eyes dancing.

'More or less,' murmured Georgina, smiling demurely.

Miles did not even hear. A group of young people were beckoning him from the other side of the marquee, and he patted Georgina's cheek ingratiatingly, excused himself and dashed off.

'I'm weary of apologising for him,' said Janus with distaste.

'You don't have to. I'm used to Miles.'

'Are you?' He turned to look down at her. 'It's odd that you've known him long enough to get used to him, and yet we know so little about you.' His voice deepened. 'But what little I could get out of Miles about you made me very eager to meet you.'

The corners of Georgina's mouth lifted in a cat-like little smile. 'Ah, but I've heard a great deal from Miles about *you*.'

'Really?' He bent closer. 'That sounds ominous.'

'Miles talks about you a lot. So much so I feel I already know you.'

Their eyes held for a long, long moment, then Janus took in a deep breath. 'It's hot in here,' he said brusquely. 'Would you care for a stroll around the garden while we wait for Katie to reappear?'

There was nothing she wanted more. Georgina was hard put to it to conceal her delight as she strolled with Janus out into the fresh air, smiling blandly in response to the incensed look Miles sent in her direction when Rosalind waylaid him as he started off in pursuit.

The marquee had been erected on what the Stanhopes used as a croquet lawn. The rest of the garden consisted of unashamedly wild shrubbery, a patch of woodland with a stream trickling through it, a couple of rockeries, and a walled kitchen garden. It took very little time to inspect.

'Not much to see,' said Janus, showing her to a secluded bench under a chestnut tree. 'But then,' he added, 'I didn't bring you out here to admire the garden.'

Georgina looked at him questioningly. 'Why *did* you bring me out here, then?'

'Apart from the obvious one of wanting to be alone with you, I'm curious to know how long you've known Miles,' he said softly.

Now how was she supposed to answer that one? Miles, as she knew very well from Harry, changed his girlfriends like other men changed their minds, so she could hardly say she'd known him since she was fourteen, when Harry had first brought him home to stay one holiday.

'Long enough,' she said, staring down at her shoes.

'My grandmother's been worried,' said Janus abruptly. 'She was convinced Miles was involved with someone totally unsuitable.'

Georgina stiffened, her chin lifting as she met the penetrating look in the dark eyes studying her. 'Unsuitable? In what way?'

He shrugged. 'Now I've actually met you it seems insulting. But for some reason my grandmother was convinced that, smitten badly though he might be, Miles's lady love was not exactly wife material.' He gave her a slow, unsettling smile. 'And having made your acquaintance, Georgina, I think she's right. You're not suitable for Miles at all.'

Georgina's pleasure in his company evaporated. 'I don't suppose I am,' she said coldly. 'My background is very different from yours.'

'That's a rather dated outlook—and wasn't what I meant at all. Are you a snob, Miss Griffiths?' he said, with a gleam of amusement in his eyes.

'No. What I meant was that my brother is the brain of the family. Unlike him, I never had any desire for academic qualifications.'

He smiled, an unsettling warmth in his eyes as he leaned closer. 'I don't suppose you did. Your particular talent, I imagine, was something you were born with.'

She shook her head, moving deliberately away from him. 'Not in the least. I've had to work hard to develop what talent I have for my calling, I assure you.'

Janus seized her hand suddenly. 'Georgina—listen. What I meant was that I firmly believe Miles is not the man for you, not the other way round. My aim is to persuade you to give him up—— '

'*What?*' Georgina withdrew her hand sharply, green flames leaping in her eyes. 'Oh, I see! You brought me out here to warn me off. Or perhaps even *buy* me off! Is that still done? What's the going price for undesirable connections like me these days?'

'You've got me all wrong, Georgina—hell and damnation!' Janus cursed bitterly under his breath, then turned with a sigh as a hand fell on his shoulder. 'Are they ready, Miles?' he went on, without turning a hair. 'I was just having a chat with—with Georgina.'

'So I see,' said Miles belligerently. 'Go and find someone else to chat up, Janus. You could keep Ros out of my hair for a start.'

Janus sprang to his feet. 'Ah, the fair Rosalind. Well, dark, really, but a very nice child, just the same. Very well. I shall exert myself to make up for your shortcomings in that direction, Miles.'

Georgina rose to her feet, wanting very badly to go home. 'Did I hear you say the bridal couple were ready to leave?' she said brightly. 'Shouldn't we speed them on their way?'

There was the usual laughter and horseplay as the bride and groom ran the gamut of confetti-hurling enthusiasts to the waiting car, which was festooned with heart-shaped silver balloons and tin cans and old boots tied to trail behind. There was a cheer as Rosalind caught the bouquet Katie tossed into the crowd, then the happy pair kissed everyone in sight one last time before they set off, and Georgina decided it was high time she did the same.

It was suddenly an enormous effort to smile and talk. She couldn't get Janus Stanhope's words out of her mind. Why wasn't she suitable for Miles? Who was he to pass judgement on anyone's eligibility! Yet, offended and disappointed though she was, she still yearned to stay just to be near him, which was so mortifying a thought she decided to remove herself from his vicinity at once. As she went with Miles to join his family Georgina realised her head was aching from tension, and the hat seemed suddenly heavy and constricting.

'It was so kind of you to ask the Harveys to invite me, Mrs Stanhope,' she said. 'I've had a lovely time, but since it's a fair drive home I think I should make a start.'

Miles looked thunderstruck. 'But, Gee, there's a little party here tonight. Didn't I say?'

'Obviously not, wretched boy!' Henrietta Stanhope gazed exasperated at her grandson. 'Surely you told Georgina we wanted her to sleep overnight?'

'Sorry, Gran—must have slipped my mind.'

Georgina smiled brightly. 'It's very sweet of you, but I couldn't anyway—must be up at dawn tomorrow, I'm afraid.'

'Early shoot?' asked Janus silkily, coming to join them.

Georgina stared at him blankly, then winced as pain shot through her head. 'I'm not used to wearing anything on my head,' she said by way of explanation and took off her hat, sighing with relief as her hair, freed from its restraint, fell tumbling about her shoulders.

'My goodness, child, that's a fine head of hair!' said Mrs Stanhope.

'But it's *red*!' exclaimed Janus.

'Of course it's red,' said his grandmother, amused. 'Creamy skin like Georgina's—not to mention the freckles—invariably comes with red hair, Janus.'

'It looked dark in the photograph——' Janus checked himself at the warning look on Miles's face.

Georgina's eyes narrowed. 'Photograph?'

'I take masses of photographs. Janus is mixing you up with someone else, Gee,' said Miles hurriedly.

Mrs Stanhope looked from one grandson to the other, then took Georgina firmly by the arm. 'I refuse to let you leave without having tea, my dear, if nothing else. Come and have a comfortable chat without the men. The caterers are serving a second round of coffee and tea in the marquee—if the wretched thing doesn't take off and sail away in this wind. The weather forecasters said nothing at all about wind today, but heaven knows we were lucky to have it sunny...'

Still talking to avoid the refusal Georgina plainly longed to make, Mrs Stanhope directed her firmly to the table where the bridegroom's mother looked up with a welcoming smile. Georgina had no choice but to sit and drink tea and chat politely while her brain wrestled with Janus's remark about a photograph. He'd thought she was the girl on the beach! She felt sick. Was *that* the reason for his instant warmth towards her? Not because he'd reciprocated her feelings in the least, but because he assumed she was someone who took her clothes off at the drop of a hat! Seething with anger, she tied back the errant hair with a length of ribbon she found in her handbag, her eyes cold as she saw Miles and Janus in the distance, deep in heated argument. Rosalind joined them to seize Miles by the hand, drawing him away as Janus came striding towards the marquee with a look of purpose.

'Tea, Janus?' asked his grandmother, her hand poised over the cups.

'Not for the moment, thanks.' Janus looked hard at Georgina. 'I wonder if I might steal Miss Griffiths away for a moment or two before she leaves.'

His grandmother looked displeased. 'Let the poor child drink her tea, darling. I've hardly exchanged a word with Georgina so far, while it seems to me you've been hogging her company most of the day.'

Miles stalked up to join them, Rosalind hotfoot behind him. 'Very true, Gran. Anyway, I think he should say his piece to Georgina in public.' Ignoring the look of thunder on his brother's face, he spoke directly to Georgina. 'Janus thought you were the girl in the photograph, Gee.'

'What *is* all this about a photograph?' demanded Mrs Stanhope.

Miles eyed her nervously. 'Well you see, Gran, I took a few shots of a friend of mine. She's a model, actually. I managed to sell one to the papers—comes out tomorrow.'

There was a buzz of excitement. Oliver Stanhope, arriving to hear the last, clapped his son on the back with enthusiasm, but Mrs Stanhope's eyes flew to Georgina, who was sitting very still, trying to pretend she wasn't there.

'But what has this to do with you, my dear?'

Georgina, wishing she were a hundred miles away, did her best to smile. 'Nothing at all, really.'

Janus's eyes narrowed to frowning slits as Rosalind took Miles by the arm eagerly.

'Have you got the photograph on you, Miles?' she said. 'Do let us see it.'

Miles, rather red in the face, glanced at his grandmother apprehensively. 'I don't really think——'

'Come along, boy,' ordered his father. 'Don't keep us in suspense.'

Janus, his face rigid with distaste, distanced himself deliberately from the rest as Miles produced the photograph from an inner pocket and handed it diffidently to his father.

'Pass it over, Oliver,' commanded Henrietta Stanhope. 'What's all the fuss—oh, I see! You thought I'd have a stroke over a naked bosom, I suppose. Splendid head of hair on the girl—not unlike Georgina's,' she added wickedly.

All eyes flew in Georgina's direction for a moment, then Miles snatched back his photograph irritably.

'Of course it isn't Georgina! The model happens to be a girl called Linda Potts, and I'm pinning my hopes on her to get my name known for me.'

Janus stared at Georgina, appalled, his mistake as to her identity written plainly on his face for an instant before it emptied of expression as Miles took her by the hand.

'Just in case anyone's still confused,' went on Miles, looking his brother in the eye, 'this is Miss Georgina Griffiths, who, as Gran and Dad already know, is the stepsister of Harry Rawlings, my room-mate up at Cambridge, and my flatmate to this day in Bayswater. I've known Georgina since—since I fell in love with her when she was a skinny little girl with pigtails, the first time I stayed with her family.'

Mrs Stanhope looked from Janus's stony face to Rosalind's stricken one and said quickly, 'Charming lad, Harry. He's stayed with us several times. Yet I'm sure he used to refer to his little sister by some other name. Am I right, dear?'

Georgina nodded ruefully. 'Carrie, probably—short for Carrots.'

Abruptly Janus came to life. '*Now* may I have a few words in private with you, Miss Griffiths? Please?'

'If you thought I was the girl in the photograph, don't apologise.' Georgina smiled brightly. 'If anything, I'm flattered. The only remote resemblance is the hair, I'm afraid—otherwise I'm hopelessly outclassed.'

'Nonsense, my dear,' said Oliver Stanhope gallantly. 'You're a very charming young woman—Miles is a lucky chap.'

Georgina gave him a tired smile. 'Thank you, Mr Stanhope. And now I really must go. I was speaking the truth about an early start tomorrow.'

'What *do* you do for a living?' asked Janus, almost as though the words were torn from him.

'She's a florist, dear,' said Mrs Stanhope, her eyes moving from her grandson's face to Georgina's with unconcealed interest.

'I part own a little shop in my home town,' added Georgina proudly, then turned away deliberately to make her round of goodbyes before allowing Miles to walk her back to her car at the Forge Garage in the early evening sunshine.

She turned on Miles fiercely once they were out of sight of the house. 'What was all that rubbish about falling in love with me when I was a child, you idiot? And why couldn't you have made it clear to—to everyone that I wasn't the girl in the photograph?'

Miles looked astonished. 'You mean Janus? Never crossed my mind he imagined you were! Anyone with half an eye could see it wasn't you, anyway. Linda's half your size for a start, Gee.'

'Thanks a lot!' said Georgina bitterly as she unlocked her car. She deposited the hat carefully on the back seat then glared up at Miles. 'Apparently Janus couldn't spot the difference——' She halted as she saw a familiar tall figure walking swiftly towards them.

'Talk of the devil,' said Miles irritably.

Miles, it seemed, was wanted on the telephone. 'Off you go—*I'll* see Miss Griffiths off,' Janus commanded, and to Georgina's intense annoyance Miles gave her a peck on the cheek, bade her a swift farewell, and took to his heels without a backward glance.

Georgina stared balefully after the retreating figure, then looked at Janus Stanhope, who stood leaning against the car, his eyes fixed on her face.

'Chelsea Flower Show,' he said abruptly, after a silence so long Georgina began to fidget.

Her heart leapt. 'Is that supposed to mean something?' she asked.

'The moment I learned you were a florist everything fell into place.' He straightened, his eyes holding hers, as though he was willing her to remember. 'We collided among the crush near the roses. You dropped your programme, I picked it up.'

'Really?' said Georgina, feigning surprise. 'Was that you?'

'I'm mortified to have made no impression on you.' But his eyes were bright with mockery, as if he knew very well she was lying. 'Odd, really,' he went on. 'The moment I saw you today I was sure I'd met you before, but because Miles had been rabbiting on about his model to me I thought I must have seen your photograph somewhere.'

'Not the one he had today,' she retorted acidly. 'The emphasis in that was not exactly on the face.'

'I know.' He smiled slowly. 'I apologise.'

'Quite unnecessary,' she muttered ungraciously, her eyes falling.

'It was a fair mistake. When Miles said he was bringing his latest girlfriend to the wedding, as my grandmother wanted, I naturally assumed it was the model. Then at first sight of you I felt there had to be a mistake. But when that hair of yours came tumbling down I felt convinced you really were the girl on the beach.'

Georgina looked at him in silence.

Janus moved closer. 'Miss Griffiths—Georgina, let me explain. I'm ten years older than Miles, and in the habit of keeping an eye on him. He's such an infant in some ways—easy prey for any little harpy with her eye on the main chance.'

Georgina's head came up, her eyes glittering like ice. 'Rest assured, Mr Stanhope, he's in no danger from me. Now, if you'll stand aside, I'd like to get in my car.'

Janus shut the Mini door with a click and leaned against it, arms folded. 'Not just yet. I'd like to put one or two things straight.'

'Mr Stanhope, I must ask you to let me into my own car!' Georgina's temper was beginning to fray. 'I've got a long way to go.'

'I won't keep you long,' he assured her. 'I just wondered if you knew that the family has always hoped Miles would marry Rosalind one day.'

Georgina opened her mouth to inform Janus Stanhope that his little brother could marry Rosalind Winter or Linda Potts, or set up a harem, for all she cared, but some inner imp of contrariness changed her mind. 'So you *are* warning me off,' she said softly.

'Only because I'm certain marriage to Miles would be disaster for you,' he said with a finality which irritated Georgina all the more because it was the absolute truth.

'Look, Mr Stanhope,' she said impatiently, 'it's my opinion that Miles should be left to marry, or cohabit with, anyone he chooses. He's twenty-five years old, not a babe in arms!'

'I still think you should give him up.' Janus moved suddenly, seizing her hand. 'Is there no way I can persuade you?'

Georgina quivered inside at his touch, the blood rising in her cheeks in response to the sudden heat in his eyes. Oh, yes, she thought, there were a hundred ways he could persuade her, and probably she'd enjoy every one. Which made no difference to the fact that he had no right to warn her—or anyone else—off marrying his precious little brother.

She removed her hand sharply. 'No. I'm not open to persuasion, Mr Stanhope.'

The glittering dark eyes held admiration as Janus Stanhope gave her a little bow very much in keeping with the formal clothes he wore. He stood away from the car, opening the door for her to get in.

'In that case, Miss Georgina Griffiths,' he said very deliberately, 'since your devotion to Miles is so unshakeable, our paths must inevitably cross again.'

CHAPTER TWO

GEORGINA suffered immense problems with her concentration on the drive home, her mind filled with all the things she should have said to Janus. Why on earth hadn't she just given in and laughed over the mistaken identity bit and confessed that she had no more romantic inclinations towards Miles than she had towards Harry?

Because, said a nasty small voice, Janus Stanhope might then have expressed his grateful thanks, bidden a fond goodbye, and Georgina Griffiths might never have laid eyes on him again in her entire life. Whereas if he thought she was still after Miles it was just possible he might contact her again to try his hand at a little more persuasion.

At this point Georgina recovered some of her usual common sense. Who was she kidding? What earthly good would it do her if he did? If Janus considered her unsuitable for his little brother, why should he feel any different from his own point of view? And yet something in his attitude seemed to indicate that he wasn't entirely indifferent to her. There was the irrefutable fact that he remembered that first chance meeting. Which indicated something. It was deeply gratifying to know that that first encounter lingered in his mind, brief though it had been. Because, like it or not, Georgina realised with dismay, she had only to conjure up that forceful face, with its crooked grin and dented nose, not to mention the duellist-style scar on the cheek, and she grew breathless and her heart began to hammer, both of which lowered the standard of her driving deplorably as she made for home along the busy motorway.

Next morning Georgina had no time for repining. After her return the previous evening she'd spent a virtually sleepless night in her flat above the shop, and crawled out of bed when her alarm went off, feeling half dead. Consequently she was in militant mood when the wholesaler arrived with the day's flowers. There was an argument most mornings, enjoyed by both sides, and after the usual uproar and haggling Georgina had begun to feel halfway human by the time her partner Chris arrived with Karen, their young assistant, in tow. Between them they stocked the front of the shop with the usual display of flowers and plants, Georgina giving a disjointed account of the wedding as they took turns to answer the telephone in the cluttered corner they grandly referred to as their office.

Christine Walters, Georgina's partner, was in her thirties, with two children away at school and a husband who travelled abroad a lot. As a result she was always thirsting for conversation as they worked together on the orders which came in both locally and nationwide for every type of floral offering for every conceivable occasion. Their young assistant Karen, a part-time student florist at the local agricultural college, saw to the customers in the front of the shop as usual, helping Georgina whenever there was a lull, while Christine divided her time between the telephone and the accounts.

Georgina was working on an outsize key for a twenty-first birthday request, marking out the form in florist's foam as she described the floral displays and the clothes worn by the guests at the wedding when Christine took an order over the phone, grinning all over her face as she listened. Georgina, the key now completed, looked up questioningly from the table decorations she was creating for the same order.

'Just listen to this!' laughed Chris. 'I've just had an order for a large bouquet of red roses to be sent to Miss Georgina Griffiths with thanks and hugs and kisses from Miles—shall I do them, or will you?'

Georgina hooted. 'What do I want with red roses? I see enough of them all day. Of course Miles would never think of that, the idiot!'

'Ungrateful girl. If you don't want the roses, send them to your mother. I'll phone them through to Hereford.'

'Great idea! Put "Thank you for the hat" on the message.'

But another offering, which arrived later in the day, met with a much warmer reception. A package addressed to Georgina revealed its contents as an exquisitely wrapped box of handmade chocolates, accompanied by a card which read,

> Flowers would be coals to Newcastle. Will you accept these instead?
>
> Janus Stanhope.

Chris and Karen were loud with excited comment before a spate of customers distracted all three, but it was much later, when the shop was closed and she was upstairs in her flat, before Georgina had any time to herself to ponder over the unexpected gift. Why had Janus felt it necessary to send her anything at all? Was he apologising for inferring she was one of the calculating harpies he'd mentioned, or for mistaking her for the girl in the photograph, or was he merely asking her to lay off Miles? She took the box of chocolates very carefully from their container, a rather smug little smile curving her mouth. One thing seemed certain. Whatever he had in mind it was clear Janus hadn't dismissed her from it the moment she'd driven away. Not, of course, that a few sweeties, handmade and expensive though they might be, were sufficient to smooth the feathers he'd ruffled very badly with his remarks on her unsuitability as a prospective sister-in-law.

Miles rang her later, to add his personal thanks to his roses, and to say that his entire family had enjoyed meeting Georgina and would like her to visit Keyne Magna again as soon as possible.

'That's very sweet of them, but not a chance, Miles. It's high time you told them the truth.'

'Er, well—could we leave it just a tiny bit longer, Gee? Gran was so taken by you it seems a shame to spoil her pleasure just yet.'

And, despite all Georgina's indignant protests, Miles won her round in the end, much against her will.

'Oh all right, but only for a few days,' she said wearily, sick of arguing at last. 'Miles, you're a pain. I'll never get embroiled in anything with you ever again, I swear it.'

The shop was very busy during the next few days, particularly at the weekend. There were three weddings to deal with on the same day, which meant providing flowers for three bridal parties, three different churches, one private house, one restaurant and one marquee. It meant working until after ten on the Friday evening, and by the time Georgina shut up shop next day she was too weary to contemplate anything other than a bath and bed, Saturday or no Saturday.

She was out of luck. As she locked up someone began banging on the shop door. She ignored it for a while, hoping whoever it was would go away, but a familiar voice began yelling her name, and with a burst of temper she flung open the outer door to Miles, her eyes flashing as she demanded what on earth he thought he was doing.

He gave her his most winning smile, managing to look guilty, sheepish and coaxing all at the same time.

'Hello, Gee. Surprise, surprise.'

'What are *you* doing here?' said Georgina, too tired for pleasantries as she locked the door. 'I thought I'd seen the last of you for a bit.'

'So did I,' he said, following her upstairs to the flat. 'I mean, I didn't think I'd need you again——' He checked himself hurriedly. 'Crumbs, that sounds terrible. Let me explain...'

'Don't tell me! Another world-shattering crisis has boiled up in your life and once again Georgina Griffiths is the one person in the universe who can help. No deal. Go away, Miles.'

'Please, Gee, don't be like that.' He took her hand, gazing earnestly into her eyes. 'Just one more tiny favour, then nothing else, ever again, I promise.'

'You said that about the wedding!'

'Well, this is still about the wedding, in a way.'

Georgina slumped down in a chair with a sigh. 'I'll regret this, I know, but go on, spit it out, Miles. What's the matter now?'

'It's Gran.' Miles sank cross-legged on the floor, looking miserable. 'She likes you, Gee.'

'I liked her too.'

He cheered visibly. 'Then perhaps you wouldn't mind sort of pretending to be the future Mrs Miles Stanhope just one more time, then.'

Georgina shot to her feet, glaring at him. 'I will *not*! What do you take me for, Miles? I gave in once because—because I'm an idiot, I suppose. But now your family know you're not presenting them with a topless little raver as your future bride there's absolutely no need for any more funny business as far as *I'm* concerned.' She stalked off to her little kitchen alcove. 'Want some tea——? Oh, answer that for me, will you?' as the telephone rang.

'Hello,' said Miles obediently into the receiver. 'Yes, this is Miss Griffiths' flat. Miles Stanhope. I *thought* it was you! What the hell do *you* want with her? What? Oh. Oh, all right. Yes. OK.'

Georgina, only half listening at the beginning, felt a sudden cold premonition as Miles put her phone down. 'Wasn't that for me?'

Miles looked hideously uncomfortable. 'It was Janus.'

Her eyes opened saucer-wide. *'Janus?'*

'He seemed a bit miffed because I was here. Said it was nothing important.'

Georgina could have thrown herself on the floor, kicking and screaming in a temper tantrum. 'Miles,' she said with dangerous calm, 'when someone rings me up I quite like to speak to whoever it is myself.'

Miles flushed. 'I know, but—but Janus rang off before I could hand you over.'

Sheer willpower shored Georgina up sufficiently to pour out cups of tea without referring to the incident again. She felt quite proud of her steely calm as she questioned Miles about his grandmother, who, it appeared, had set her heart not only on a trip to Ascot on Ladies' Day the following week, but on having Miles bring his charming Georgina along to enjoy a champagne picnic with the family.

'No way!' said Georgina at once, sounding anything but charming.

'Oh, Gee, please! She really does have a frightfully dodgy ticker, you see,' said Miles anxiously. 'Likely to pop off at any time. So please say you'll come, just to humour the old darling. She took to you in a big way, you know. Said you had spirit. Besides, this might well be Gran's last Ascot. We don't want anything to spoil it for her.'

How, thought Georgina, as she saw him off later, could she have said no? Besides, she admitted to her innermost self, by saying yes to a family outing it was highly probable she'd run into Janus again, which, if she were honest, had influenced her decision rather a lot. Once reluctant consent was wrung out of her, however, she'd sent Miles packing, firmly quashing any hopes he might have entertained about supper.

Left in peace at last Georgina fumed impotently, cursing the fate which had arranged for Miles to answer the phone the one time Janus should hit on to ring her. She ate an omelette without tasting a mouthful of it as she sat at her dormer window, in no mood to appreciate the glitter of flamingo pink on the river as the sun sank behind the hills beyond the town. Now, of course, Janus would be firmly convinced she was being bloody-minded about Miles—probably heartily sorry he'd wasted his money on the chocolates.

She sighed heavily, then had a bath and went to bed, expecting to lie awake all night.

Having fallen asleep the moment her head touched the pillow, Georgina surfaced groggily next morning to the shrill of the telephone, managing to knock the receiver on the floor before finally gathering her wits sufficiently to answer it, her teeth grinding together as she saw the time.

'If you keep on doing this, Miles,' she hissed furiously, 'I'll never *speak* to you again, let alone come to Ascot.'

There was a pause at the other end of the line.

'At the risk of disappointing you,' drawled a very different voice from Miles's light tones, 'I'm afraid this is the other Stanhope—Janus.'

Georgina sat bolt upright, her eyes goggling.

'Are you still there?' he demanded.

'Yes.'

'Good. I thought I'd be luckier at catching you alone at this hour than I was last night. From your greeting I gather Miles is no longer there.'

Georgina, teeth gritted, counted to ten. 'No. He's not. Nor is anyone else,' she added sweetly. 'It's very early—or perhaps you hadn't noticed.'

'Sorry I woke you. I thought you might be going out. I wanted a word with you after ringing off so abruptly last night.'

'Did you? Miles didn't say.'

'I was—rather annoyed to find him with you.'

'Why?'

'Don't be naïve, Miss Griffiths. You know perfectly well I think you're all wrong for Miles.'

'Perhaps you should tell Miles this, not me, Mr Stanhope.'

'I have. Miles is being distinctly mulish on the subject.'

Georgina settled back against her pillows. 'Good for Miles! But surely you haven't rung—twice—merely to harangue me about my lamentable ineligibility?'

'What long words you use, Georgina!' he mocked. 'And of course you're right. My motive for ringing—on both occasions—was to say I happen to be in your area this weekend. I hoped I might take you out to a meal, or even a drink if that's all the time you can spare.'

There was nothing of Miles's cajolery in Janus Stanhope's voice. He made his request with the assurance of a man certain of his answer.

Georgina, ignoring an inner voice which urged her to say yes to anything he asked, refused politely. 'I'm afraid I can't, Mr Stanhope. I'm off to Hereford to spend the day with my family.'

'All day?'

'All day.'

'Couldn't you get back in time for just one drink later tonight?'

Pride salvaged, Georgina pretended to think it over. 'I suppose I could,' she said at last. 'But not until nine at the earliest.'

'Fine. Shall I come and collect you, or will you meet me here in the bar? I'm at the Unicorn.'

'I'll see you there,' she said, and rang off to stare at the ceiling, not sure how she felt now Janus Stanhope had actually made contact. What did he want? Did he imagine personal persuasion might unfasten her claws from poor innocent little Miles? She smiled, stretching luxuriously. If he only knew! Poor Miles was merely the unsuspecting decoy. Her quarry, she thought, eyes sparkling, was Janus Stanhope, not his little brother. The refusal to let Miles out of her so-called clutches had worked like a charm, after all. Janus was stepping up his efforts to separate her from his brother just as she'd hoped. Perfect.

For once her day in the bosom of her family crawled by for Georgina. By the time she was ready to leave her mother made it plain she was heartily sorry her child had put Miles Stanhope's celebrated brother off until so late. Bidden by her exasperated parent to weed a flower bed or two to channel her energies, Georgina got through the afternoon by taking a busman's holiday among her mother's flowers then spent a couple of hours getting ready, fiddling with her newly washed hair until it shone like molten copper. Once brushed and scented and groomed to a hair's breadth, she arrayed herself in her favourite ink-blue lawn dress, hugged her amused parents, then set off in her Mini to keep her unexpected appointment.

After a few minutes in her flat to check with her mirror, Georgina set out on foot for the short walk to the Unicorn, suddenly almost paralysed by nerves as she approached the hotel. It was an old posting house, with a solid air of comfort popular with travellers and locals alike, and, as usual in the evenings, the bar was crowded. The moment Georgina arrived in the doorway Janus sprang up from a table in one of the window embrasures, tall and striking in a mushroom corduroy jacket, striped shirt, and heavy khaki cotton drill trousers. He smiled, his eyes lighting up at the sight of her, and Georgina felt suddenly very young and uncertain as she watched him make his way through the crowd towards her.

'Good evening. You're late, Georgina,' he said, as he took her hand.

'Really?' She smiled. 'Only a few minutes, surely!'

'Minutes to you, hours to me!' He led her to his table, seating her with her face to the light and her back to the room. 'There,' he remarked. 'Now I can look at you at my leisure, and no one else is afforded the same privilege. What would you like to drink?'

Georgina, annoyed to find herself shy, marshalled her forces sufficiently to request a glass of white wine, then watched Janus at the bar from the corner of her eye as he ordered it, wondering if this new, head-on type of approach was his latest ploy to detach her from Miles. If so, it was very enjoyable, she decided, giving him a warm smile as he set the glass in front of her.

'Thank you. Have you been here long?'

'Since last night. I stayed overnight.'

Georgina sat stunned. Janus, actually here in town all this time unknown to her!

'I had business in the neighbourhood,' he went on, 'so I decided to stop over and renew my acquaintance with you.' Janus drank some of the Scotch in his glass, eyeing her over the rim. 'I rang you last night to ask you out to lunch, dinner, whatever you wanted. But got Miles instead of you.'

'He came to wheedle me into going to Ascot with your family.'

'Was he successful?'

'Yes.'

There was silence while Janus Stanhope studied the composed girl beside him, his eyes lingering with overt pleasure on her face as the setting sun lent a glow to Georgina's cream-pale skin, striking sparks of fire from the bronze-red curls caught back with a navy velvet bow at the nape of her neck.

'Are you always this quiet, Georgina?' he asked.

She raised her eyes to his. 'No. I'm not. I've been wondering what possible reason you can have for asking me out.'

Janus leaned back, relaxed, a smile in his eyes. 'My dear Georgina, since it seems we're soon to be related, surely it's only natural I should want to know you better!'

She smiled. 'Why, of course! I hadn't thought of that.'

'Possibly because you have no intention of becoming my sister-in-law?' he said silkily.

Very true, thought Georgina with a secret shudder. She could imagine nothing more unbearable. 'Now why should you think that?' she said aloud.

'You don't behave like a girl in love.'

Georgina was relieved to hear it. She must be a better actress than she thought. 'I'm not the type,' she assured him. 'Besides, I've known Miles too long to be starry-eyed about him.'

'Ros has known him even longer,' said Janus swiftly, 'and she's unfailingly starry-eyed about the idiot. Of course, she's very young,' he added reflectively.

No younger than me, thought Georgina acidly, and changed the subject to her invitation to Ascot with the Stanhopes.

'I'm looking forward to it immensely,' she fibbed brightly. 'I haven't been before.'

'Don't you care for racing?'

'I've never thought much about it. There's a racecourse right here, but all it's ever meant to me was more of a crush in the town on race-meeting Saturdays.' She shrugged. 'Ascot's different, of course. I'll enjoy looking at the hats as much as the horses—and I'm looking forward to seeing the Queen and the rest of the Royal Family.'

'How about your shop?'

'My mother's volunteered to fill in for me again. I'm afraid I'm really taking advantage of her lately. Luckily Thursday's early closing day.'

Janus gave her a wry smile. 'I blush to think of my gaffe, when you said your mother stood in for you when you needed time off.'

Georgina's eyes danced, taking on some of the blue of her dress as they sparkled at him. 'I forgot to tell her about that. She'll be tickled pink at being taken for a part-time topless model!'

Janus shuddered. 'For heaven's sake don't breathe a word—particularly to your father, or he'll never allow me to cross his threshold.'

There was a pause while they looked at each other consideringly.

'Had you expected to?' asked Georgina.

He stood up, collecting her empty glass. 'Of course. Since we're about to become relatives I'd say it's inevitable.'

Georgina scowled at his back as he walked across to the bar, judging from the slight swagger in his step that he felt he'd scored yet another direct hit.

The short period left before closing time passed in what seemed to Georgina like the twinkling of an eye as she chatted away quite happily about her work and some of the rather bizarre confections she was required to make on occasion, particularly for funerals.

A shadow passed over Janus's face. 'I hope not to have recourse to anything similar yet awhile.'

Georgina's heart smote her. 'Your grandmother, you mean? I thought she looked in remarkably good shape at the wedding.'

He shrugged. 'She's a game lady, all right, but the utter despair of her doctor. If she feels like doing something she goes right ahead and does it, regardless of her heart condition.'

Georgina looked thoughtful. 'I can understand that. Perhaps she feels what life she has left to her wouldn't be worth living if she lived it as an invalid.'

Warmth lit Janus Stanhope's dark eyes as he smiled at her. 'You're right, of course. Nevertheless, Ascot straight on top of the wedding verges on the rash! Not that there's a blind bit of use trying to stop her. She's such a tartar about having her own way all we can do is humour her and try to see she doesn't get overtired, or upset in any way.'

Which, thought Georgina, is my sole reason for repeating my triumphant performance as Miles's fiancée, fool that I am. She looked across at him questioningly.

'Tell me what exactly it is that you do, Janus—I'm curious to learn what a man like you does in a bank.'

'A man like me,' he repeated, his eyes narrowing. 'What, exactly, does that mean?'

'Nothing untoward,' she assured him. 'It's just that you give the impression of doing something more physical for a living, somehow.'

'Whereas all the rough stuff I engage in goes on in the corridors of power!' he said with mock drama, then shrugged. 'I'm with one of the major British merchant banks—nothing terribly exciting, I'm afraid. My field is corporate finance. I head a small team handling anything from aggressive take-overs to privatisation projects.'

Georgina was rather annoyed to find herself impressed. 'It all sounds terribly high-powered and glamorous—and a far cry from life in this neck of the woods.'

'Sometimes I think I'm mad not to get out of the rat race and find something in just such a neck of the woods, Georgina,' he said, surprising her. 'Life in the big city is hellishly demanding. So far I enjoy the cut and thrust. When I don't I'll move out and do something more peaceful—throw pots, or write my memoirs.'

Georgina laughed, shaking her head. 'I can't picture it somehow. Besides, you don't abandon the rat race. You just exchange one kind for another.'

Janus regarded her with respect. 'Such words of wisdom from one so young. How old *are* you, by the way?'

'Twenty.   Almost   twenty-one,'   confessed Georgina reluctantly, feeling her cheeks grow warm at the shock on her companion's attractive face.

Janus looked thunderstruck. 'Is that *all*? Good grief, you're a mere infant! Somehow I thought you were the same age as Miles, at least. When he said he'd known you forever I got the impression you were contemporaries.'

Georgina shook her head, smiling as she told him she was a skinny, freckled fourteen the first time Harry brought Miles home, an occasion marked by a fall from an apple tree when Miles egged her on to pick fruit from the highest branch. On the next visit he'd taken her rowing on the river and over-turned the boat.

'Our river's tidal here, of course,' she said, chuckling. 'Not very much like the Cam, as Miles explained when he returned me, drenched, to my mother.' She glanced at her watch and finished her drink hurriedly. 'Goodness, I must go. It's late.' She looked at him questioningly. 'Are you driving back to London tonight?'

'No, my child,' he said, pulling out her chair for her. 'I'd rather drive at first light when the roads are empty.'

Georgina walked with him through the still-crowded bar, smiling at several acquaintances as she passed. When they reached the foyer she held out her hand. 'Thank you. That was very pleasant. Goodnight.'

Janus took the hand and tucked it through his arm. 'Not a bit of it, Miss Griffiths. I shall deliver you, safe and sound, to wherever it is you live before I turn in.'

Georgina had no objection at all. It was no distance to her little shop at the crown of the steep main road of the town, and she could easily and quite safely have walked it alone. But it fitted in beautifully with her plans for taming Janus Stanhope to have him at her side as they strolled through the warm, summer night, where a faint afterglow of sunset still edged the sky on the far side of the river.

'By the way, why *were* you at the Chelsea Flower Show?' she asked.

He gave her a smiling, sidelong glance. 'Fate must have sent me—to meet you!'

Georgina favoured him with an ironic little smile. 'Very pretty,' she said drily. 'What was the real reason?'

'Need you ask? I was escorting my intrepid grandmother.' Janus shook his head. 'She seems intent on packing everything she can into this summer—would you think me fanciful if I said it's something which disturbs me?'

'Not fanciful at all. I understand only too well.' Which was true enough, she thought. Otherwise nothing would have persuaded her to carry on with her ridiculous charade as Miles's fiancée.

'You, I take it,' said Janus, 'were there in a professional capacity.'

'Yes. But I've been lots of times, long before I decided flowers were to be my career. Mother regards Chelsea as the high point of her summer calendar. She loves gardening, but Dad prefers golf, so I've always gone with her to the Flower Show. These days, of course, it's of professional interest to me.' She gave him a sidelong look beneath her lashes. 'Quite a coincidence that we should bump into each other there.'

'Not coincidence, Georgina. As I said before, it must have been fate.' This time there was no smile on his face as he looked down at her, and Georgina looked away, conscious of treading in temptingly dangerous territory again.

'What I fail to understand,' said Janus, as they wandered slowly up the hill past shuttered shops and silent banks, 'is why, to revert to your account of your experiences at Miles's hands, you can even contemplate *any* kind of relationship with him, let alone marriage.'

Georgina opened her mouth to explain, then shut it again. Not yet. 'I'm fond of him,' she said at last, which was no more than the truth. She *was* fond of him, in much the same way she was fond of her brother Harry. But since she'd promised Miles to carry on with the silly masquerade for a bit she could hardly tell Janus that. 'We've known each other a long time.'

'Hm. Ever since he fell in love with a kid in pigtails.' Janus sounded sceptical. 'Funny he's kept so quiet about it until now.'

Georgina thought quickly. 'Well we've both had other—other relationships over the years, you see——'

'What years? You're only a child!'

'I'm not!' she retorted, stung, 'I'm a grown woman, a partner in a successful little business, remember.' With a faint suggestion of flounce she turned into the little alley alongside the shop premises. Janus strolled after her, waiting as she unlocked the door.

'Take my advice, Georgina,' he said very softly. 'Forget all about Miles. Believe me—he's not for you.'

She hesitated, sorely tempted to tell him the truth. 'I think you should leave that for Miles and me to sort out,' she said at last, suddenly breathless as he moved so close she could feel the warmth of him through her thin cotton dress.

'May I come in?' he asked abruptly.

She shook her head. 'No. This is a small town. The time of your return to the Unicorn will be duly logged, I assure you.'

He sighed. 'A pity. Goodnight then, Georgina.'

'Goodnight.' As she opened the door she couldn't resist the question she'd been longing to ask all evening. She turned to look up at him. 'Why *did* you stay on here today, Janus?'

He smiled deep into her eyes. 'I would have thought it was obvious. I put up with a lonely Saturday night, and a boring, frustrating Sunday, just for the pleasure of a couple of hours in your company tonight, Georgina.'

Heat surged in her face, indiscernible behind the creamy skin which never displayed any colour other than its freckles, something Georgina had cause to be thankful for on occasion. She smiled shakily, feeling suddenly young and overwhelmed in the company of this sophisticated, disturbing man.

'I—I forgot,' she stammered. 'To thank you for the chocolates, I mean. Not that an offering of any kind was necessary.'

Janus leaned indolently against the wall. 'I felt I'd offended you badly in some way—probably because I mistook you for the type of girl who takes her clothes off to make a living. Personally I see nothing wrong in it at all if a girl has the necessary attributes, but I fancy you were pretty unhappy about my mistake. Am I right?'

'Yes,' she admitted.

'So, since it seemed silly to send flowers to a florist, I sent sweets to the sweet instead.' He pushed himself away from the wall, giving her the very unusual feeling of having a man tower over her.

Georgina backed away. 'Oh. Well—thank you. They were delicious, and much appreciated—by me *and* my colleagues.'

His hand shot out to imprison hers, and Georgina stood rigid, every nerve tingling at the contact.

'Don't well-brought-up little girls give donors of presents a kiss by way of thanks?' he said, so quietly Georgina wasn't sure she'd heard him properly, and leaned nearer to catch the words, a reaction he interpreted as consent and kissed her, pulling her into his arms at the precise moment she realised it was what she'd been wanting him to do from the moment she'd first set eyes on him.

Georgina, for several reasons unable to think very clearly, noted, dazed, that the shock from the touch of Janus Stanhope's hand was nothing at all to that of his mouth as it met hers. Her blood seemed to roar through her veins in a rushing tide of response, her knees buckled, she sagged against him and his arms tightened instinctively, holding her close against him. His mouth grew urgent, her lips parted, his tongue slid into her mouth, and the answering fire which blazed up inside her frightened Georgina out of her wits. She tore herself away, breathing raggedly as she stared at him with eyes which burned darkly in her pale face.

'They must have been very expensive chocolates,' she said unsteadily.

'The kiss was sweeter by far,' he said caressingly, and seized her again by the shoulders. 'No—don't jump away. I'm not going to kiss you again. Not for the moment, anyway.' The faint light from the street lamp in the outside world caught the glitter in his eyes as they held hers. 'Is that how you kiss Miles, Georgina? Is it?'

On the point of saying she'd never kissed Miles in her life, and had no intention of doing so in the future, either, Georgina took in a deep, shaky breath and freed herself from his grasp. 'That—that's nothing to do with you.'

'I beg to differ.' Janus moved back, what she could see of his face oddly forbidding. 'Georgina, if a woman of mine responded to another man like that I'd lock her up out of harm's way.'

'Since I'm not your woman the subject doesn't arise,' she pointed out tartly, and opened her door. 'Goodnight. Thank you for the drink.'

'Goodnight, Georgina. Sweet dreams,' he said softly. 'See you at Ascot.'

'You're coming too?' she asked before she could stop herself.

'Now I know you'll be there wild horses wouldn't keep me away!'

CHAPTER THREE

WHEN Miles rang Georgina the following evening he was not at all pleased to hear Janus had taken her out for a drink.

'What the blazes is he playing at?' he said wrathfully. 'I know he's sort of between women at the moment but you're nothing like the type he usually fancies, Gee.'

Georgina bristled. She'd spent a very abstracted Monday trying to forget Janus Stanhope's kisses, and failed so dismally that Chris and Karen were convinced she was sickening for something. Miles's remarks touched on nerves already exposed, one way and another. 'Of course I'm not his type,' she snapped. 'He thinks I'm your fiancée, remember, Miles Stanhope—though how anyone could believe it when I'm not even sporting a ring, I can't imagine.'

'I never thought of that!'

'That's your trouble—you just don't think, period.'

Miles, plainly alarmed Georgina might refuse to come to Ascot after all, hastily began winning her round, insisting her presence was absolutely vital. His grandmother, he said with gloom, had made a complete mess of things by inviting Ros, who was taking a day off from her brats to make one of the party.

'So I need you badly as my cover, Gee,' he said urgently. 'Gran says come and stay the night at Keyne Magna beforehand, then travel to Ascot in the Rolls.'

Georgina thought this over. 'Will you be there?'

'At home? Yes. Janus can't get away until next day, so he'll meet us at Ascot.'

'It's very kind of Mrs Stanhope. Tell her I'll be delighted,' said Georgina, promising to be in Keyne Magna in time for a late cold supper two days later.

It was a tired Georgina who set off late the following Wednesday. Feeling guilty over more time off at one of the peak busy times, she'd worked herself to dropping point before shutting up shop. Fortunately the volume of traffic on the motorway had diminished by the time she headed into Wiltshire with the sunset at her back, and she began to unwind once the first busy junctions were left behind as the road began to curve through the hillier countryside around Bath. She reached Keyne Magna just as the sun was setting. And this time, with more attention to spare for its charm, Georgina was enchanted with Glebe House. Sturdily tranquil within its sheltering walls, it gave out an air of welcome which the sunset augmented by painting the gabled roof and stone walls with a wash of rose light. Then the peace was shattered as Miles came hurtling from the house to kiss Georgina's cheek.

'Gran's watching,' he muttered, and grabbed her hand surreptitiously, thrusting a ring on her third finger in such haste she squeaked in protest. 'There—will that do?'

Georgina had no time to pass an opinion, since Henrietta Stanhope appeared almost at once in the doorway to welcome the visitor.

'Come along in, my dear,' she called, smiling. 'How nice to see you again. Miles, you bring Georgina's things—and careful with that hat box!'

Georgina was borne into the house on a wave of warmth and welcome as Oliver Stanhope added his greetings, then Madge, the cheerful, friendly housekeeper, led her up shallow oaken stairs to a pretty room with a view of the back garden and church tower from its window. Left to herself for a moment, Georgina felt a sudden dart of pain as she examined the ring Miles had pushed on her finger. It was charming, set with a green stone she thought might be a beryl, surrounded by diamond chips. But it worsened her pangs of guilt, making it seem more of a sin than before to pose as the fiancée of the son of the house—particularly when it was the wrong son. If she were here as Janus's intended bride, now...

Dismissing the thought as sheer fantasy, Georgina hung up the new dress she'd bought for Ladies' Day, then changed from trousers and shirt into the blue cotton dress worn for Janus, her breath catching as she relived the moments in his arms for the hundredth time, then she put him firmly from her mind, and went downstairs to join the others for supper.

The evening passed very pleasantly. The Stanhopes, intent on making up for the lack of opportunity to talk to Georgina at the wedding, soon learned all about the thriving little flower shop and her family, that Philip Griffiths was an accountant and had married Georgina's mother when she had been a young widow with a baby son, Harry.

'Ah, yes—steady sort of chap, young Harry.' Oliver Stanhope gave his son a significant look. 'Damn good influence on Miles, here.' He smiled kindly at Georgina. 'Now you're prepared to take on Miles as well, my dear. Keep it in the family, so to speak.'

At which point, to Georgina's dismay, the conversation turned to the question of a possible wedding date, whereupon Miles made vague noises about not having settled anything yet, and changed the subject hastily to the arrangements for the following day.

'My dear, you look very pale,' said Mrs Stanhope, concerned.

'It's been a long day,' confessed Georgina, resigned to the fact that her freckles were probably standing out like ink blots at the mere mention of a wedding.

'Then go to bed, child. It's likely to be a long day tomorrow, too.'

'Very true,' said Oliver Stanhope with a frown. 'I only hope it won't be too much for you, Mother.'

'Of course it won't, will it, Gran?' said Miles cheerfully, jumping up. 'Come on, Gee, you look whacked. Time for bye-byes.'

Georgina woke very early next morning, filled with a singing sense of anticipation which puzzled her for a moment as she gazed at the bright blue sky from the unfamiliar window. Then it dawned on her that her excitement stemmed from the thought of seeing Janus Stanhope again. She stretched luxuriously, then winced as she saw the unfamiliar ring on her finger. When Janus caught sight of *that* little bauble would he turn away in disgust and ignore her, or would he redouble his efforts to separate her from Miles?

The picnic the Stanhopes had organised for Ladies' Day at Ascot was like no other in Georgina's experience. To indulge his mother's whim Oliver Stanhope had hired a Rolls Bentley limousine for the day, complete with chauffeur. This way, he explained with a grin over breakfast, he'd be able to enjoy the odd glass of champagne or two himself without worrying about the drive home. When Georgina heard the picnic lunch was in the hands of professional caterers, she chuckled. Picnics, for her, she confessed, were usually of the sandwiches and lemonade variety. Mrs Stanhope assured Georgina that today's affair was very much outside the norm for them, too.

'It's a special treat to celebrate my birthday,' she explained.

'It's not your birthday today!' said Georgina in dismay.

'No, no, dear. Not for a couple of weeks. But I insisted on the picnic as a birthday present.' The dark eyes gleamed wickedly. 'Oliver's always afraid I won't be here for another year, so he tends to indulge me in whatever I want. Last year my request was fairly modest, so this year I'm making up for it with the trip to Ascot!'

By ten they were on their way, Henrietta Stanhope in a printed filmy dress with loose matching coat, Georgina in Liberty lawn in a tawny print to match the pair of tortoiseshell butterflies on her wide-brimmed hat, which, for some reason she didn't care to examine too closely, she had felt obliged to buy for the occasion, citing the unusual heat as her excuse, because she'd felt too hot in the one worn to the wedding. Neither Oliver Stanhope nor Miles had been obliged to hire clothes for the occasion. Mr Stanhope's morning suit, he told Georgina with a smug look at his waistline, was the same one he'd been married in, though it was a bit more of a squeeze these days. Miles, however, who was as thin as a rake, was a wonderful sight to behold, decked in his old Eton tail suit, kingfisher brocade waistcoat, a multi-coloured Hermès tie and the grey Hilhouse top hat handed down from his grandfather.

'I feel like a dowdy hen alongside a gorgeous peacock,' laughed Georgina as he handed her into the car.

Miles preened outrageously. 'I look *very* pretty, don't I?'

The day was cloudless and sunny, and promised to be hotter as the chauffeur drove to the village of Nadderford a few miles away to pick up Rosalind. As Miles dashed out of the car to collect the latter, Mrs Stanhope expressed the hope that Georgina wasn't upset by having Rosalind along on the trip.

Georgina was able to reassure her with complete truth that she didn't mind in the least, happy at the thought that with Rosalind to dog Miles's footsteps it seemed all the more likely Janus might feel obliged to dance attendance on herself.

Rosalind ducked into the car, looking very pretty in a flower-printed blue dress, a white cartwheel straw hat in her hand. She gave breathless apologies for holding them up, then perched on the tip-up seat alongside Miles, smiling diffidently at Georgina, who gave the girl a reassuring smile in return to show she bore no ill will.

There was much talk of horses as the limousine sped along country roads in the sunshine before joining the busy motorway, where the younger members of the party made a game of spotting the other cars bound for Ascot. All racebound vehicles were easily identifiable by the extravagant hats lying out of harm's way not only on back windows of large limousines, but in smaller sportier vehicles speeding along in the sunshine, all with Ascot as their goal.

Georgina found herself caught up in the excitement as they turned off the motorway and began the long, slow drive towards Ascot itself, at one stage passing an open coach drawn by four matched horses, the vehicle crammed to bursting point with young men dressed like Miles and girls clutching wide-brimmed hats as their splendid conveyance bowled along.

It was almost noon when the Rolls arrived at its destination. The driver parked the car among several very like it, slotting it in with dexterity between a Rolls Corniche and another Rolls Bentley, in a space where the caterers had already set up a trestle table covered with snowy damask set not only with sparkling crystal and silver, but even, to Georgina's astonishment, with vases of flowers and an awning overhead to keep off the unusually fierce noonday sun.

'Ninety degrees forecast today,' observed Mr Stanhope, as he helped his mother into a com-

fortable folding chair under one of the large um-
brellas produced from the boot. 'Now, then, ladies,
hats on, or you'll get sunstroke before you've even
managed to place a bet!'

Georgina sat happily under an umbrella with her
glass of Bucks fizz, thoroughly enjoying the
colourful scene as she watched the passing show of
haute couture fashion. Ros, once she realised
Georgina bore no animosity towards her, displayed
an astringent sense of humour, and they both enjoyed themselves thoroughly as they awarded points
out of ten to the outfits, some of which, according
to Henrietta Stanhope, would have done better to
be less flagrantly revealing.

'It's regrettable,' she declared, eyeing a plump
young girl in a backless white lace mini-dress, 'that
the merest suggestion of a heatwave prompts such
a vulgar display of bare flesh.'

Miles and his father disagreed shamelessly, saying
that from their point of view it merely added to the
general enjoyment of a splendid British tradition.

Georgina had convinced herself Janus wasn't
going to turn up by the time he came strolling into
sight, looking so elegant in his black morning coat
with his black silk top hat tilted low over his eyes
that he quite eclipsed the peacock showiness of his
sibling. His waistcoat was charcoal brocade, his tie
garnet silk, and he wore a white gardenia in his
lapel, the whole effect one of such effortless el-
egance that Georgina was struck temporarily dumb.
No one noticed it in the flurry of greetings as Janus
raised his hat to kiss his grandmother, touched an
affectionate finger to Rosalind's cheek, then came
to a halt in front of Georgina, who gave him her

hand to shake, since she felt the occasion required something more than a mere smile by way of greeting.

Janus took her hand in his, the trace of intimacy in the smile he gave her enough for Miles to eye his brother with rancour as he bore him off to ply him with champagne, saying they were all starving and would Janus kindly swallow his drink quickly so they could get on with lunch?

At the meal Georgina sat between Miles and Janus to enjoy chilled salmon and lobster, with generous slices of crust-encased Beef Wellington for those of a heartier appetite, like Miles, who for all his string-bean physique possessed an astonishing capacity for food. As she watched Henrietta Stanhope's overt pleasure in her birthday treat Georgina's guilt over her ongoing masquerade began to subside a little, and she settled down to take full advantage of a treat unlikely to come her way very often.

They were halfway through lunch when she became aware of a warm, hard pressure all along one leg, her pulse accelerating as she realised the contact was deliberate. The warmth from Janus Stanhope's muscular thigh, through striped trouser leg and thin skirt, distracted her very effectively from her contribution to the discussion on likely winners for the afternoon's races. The table was small. To move away meant Georgina would be jammed up against Miles, who, though not of a romantic inclination towards her, was nevertheless all male and likely to misunderstand. On the other hand she had no intention of allowing Janus to think the kisses of the other evening gave him licence for further familiarity. She sat still for a moment, while Janus chatted to his grandmother without betraying by the flicker of an eyelash that he was causing havoc with his other companion under cover of the starched cloth. Very slowly and carefully, Georgina raised one foot slightly, moved it so that it hovered over Janus's, then lowered it so that her slender, three-inch heel ground cruelly into his instep, just above his shoe, while at the same time she carried on a discussion with the waiter on the rival merits of raspberry meringue or *tarte au citron* for pudding.

'Something wrong, Janus?' asked Mrs Stanhope, noting her grandson's sharp intake of breath.

He blinked, smiling rather fixedly. 'Twinge of indigestion—gone now.'

Later, once Henrietta Stanhope was installed in the box owned by Janus's bank, and they were all waiting for the royal procession to come into view, Janus moved unobtrusively so that he stood directly behind Georgina.

'I may never walk normally again,' he whispered into the nape of her neck.

Georgina ignored him, keeping her eyes firmly on the colourful throng below as everyone strained for the first glimpse of the royal party. Pretending she hadn't heard, she moved closer to Miles, which wasn't all that easy in such a wide-brimmed hat. Miles, who was craning his neck to see into the distance, never even noticed. Fine sort of fiancé he is, thought Georgina bitterly. Suddenly there was a fanfare, a great cheer went up and applause sounded all along the rails of Tattersalls below and from the Heath on the other side of the track, as the first landau came in sight bearing the Queen and the Duke of Edinburgh, in company with Prince Charles and one of the royal dukes. Georgina stood on tiptoe, filled with excitement and a sudden rush of patriotic pride at the strains of the national anthem. She clapped enthusiastically with the rest as the trotting horses bore the royal party to the entrance to the royal enclosure, all feminine eyes drawn like magnets to the clothes worn by the royal ladies.

'Don't they look stunning,' sighed Rosalind. 'Come on, Georgina—just time to get a bet on before the first race.'

Janus refused to let Miles give the girls any advice on likely winners, and showed them how to study form on the race card to draw their own conclusions. Rosalind, dismissing this method as far too dull, chose the horse with the prettiest name, but Georgina ran an eye over the previous performances of the runners in the first race, noted which horses were suited to the hard going of the day's race-meeting and queued to put her money on her choice, refusing to let either Miles or Janus perform the service for her.

'This is all a great novelty,' she said, laughing, 'so please let me do it all myself.'

Georgina's father had delighted her by giving her money to spend, telling her not to be disappointed if she lost the lot, but to regard it as the price for a splendid day out. With suppressed excitement she handed over a sixth of her allowance for the day, betting on a win, but keeping the name of her horse to herself as they returned to watch the race from the box.

With Rosalind bobbing up and down beside her in excitement, Georgina hung on to her hat with one hand as she peered down the course to watch the horses come in sight to the accompaniment of a rising crescendo of sound from the stands as every punter at the meeting roared out encouragement. At first it seemed a cut and dried win for the favourite, but as the horses swept level with the box, sun glinting on the gaudy colours of the jockeys' silks, Georgina let out a shriek of pure elation, jumping up and down in wild excitement as her horse moved up from fourth to third, then to second, and then, just by a nose, flew past the finishing post to snatch the race from the favourite.

She spun round to clutch Miles, crying 'I won, I won!' and he crowed with delight and swept her off to claim her prize.

Putting her father's money away, Georgina used some of her winnings to bet on not only a win for the heavily backed favourite in the next race, but on a place bet for another horse by the name of Floral Tribute, a name she felt unable to pass up, if only for sentimental reasons.

This time the entire party had money on the favourite. There was universal euphoria as it won by three lengths, as expected, but with Floral Tribute, totally unexpectedly, coming in second.

'You don't mean to say you bet on that, too,' said Janus, laughing at Georgina's jubilation.

'Well, well, child,' said Oliver Stanhope in great amusement. 'What odds did you get?'

'Thirty-three to one,' said Georgina happily, and Henrietta Stanhope shook her head, laughing.

'You'd better watch this one, Miles, or she'll lose your shirt for you once you're married!'

There was an awkward little pause as Rosalind looked suddenly stricken, then Janus took Georgina briskly by the arm.

'Come on. I'll help you carry your winnings.'

He kept his hand beneath her elbow as he piloted her through the crowd to collect her loot, then suggested they take a look at the horses as they paraded before the next race. Georgina assented readily, her spirits rocketing again. It was all too easy to forget the silly little conspiracy which had brought her here to Ascot as she strolled through the elegant, colourful crowd with Janus Stanhope who, even allowing for her own personal prejudice, was a match for any of the top-hatted, tail-coated men in sight. Suddenly Georgina clutched him by the arm and stood stock still, her eyes like saucers as she saw the Prince and Princess of Wales returning to the Royal Enclosure on the way back from inspecting the runners for the next race.

'Doesn't she look beautiful?' sighed Georgina.

'So do you,' returned Janus, and bent to peer under the brim of her hat with a smile which, although it quickened her pulse, also recalled her to the fact that they ought to be joining the others.

Janus disagreed, saying he fancied a drink, then a look at the runners for the next race. After providing Georgina with iced fresh orange juice, he took her to watch the parade of glossy, thoroughbred horseflesh, her delight in the scene, combined with her pleasure in Janus's company, proving far more important than betting on the next race, which they watched together from the rails, since it was too late to get back to the others in time for the start.

As the winner swept past the post Georgina grinned up at Janus.

'Not nearly so exciting if you don't bet!'

He shook his head in mock reproof, taking her hand in his. 'I only hope we haven't set you on the road to ruin, young lady.' He paused, frowning, then lifted her hand to look at the ring on her finger. 'This is new,' he said austerely.

Georgina looked down at the modest little ring rather as though she'd never seen it before. 'Oh. Yes. Miles only gave it to me last night.'

'Where did he get it—in a Christmas cracker?'

'That's unkind!'

Janus raised her hand to his lips, holding her eyes as he did so. 'You deserve far better, Georgina.'

'What the hell are you playing at, Janus?' said an angry voice behind them and Georgina swung round to face Miles, who was glaring at his brother with uncharacteristic hostility.

Janus shrugged, unperturbed. 'Just about to bring Georgina back, old son.'

'About bloody time too,' snapped Miles, seizing Georgina by the arm. 'Come *on*, Gee, the others are waiting to have tea.'

'You're hurting me,' she protested, as Miles hauled her off through the crowds, deliberately leaving Janus behind.

'You're supposed to be with me,' Miles hissed in her ear. 'What's the point of coming along as my fiancée, then swanning off with Janus, for Pete's sake? *I'm* the one Gran's making threatening noises to, not him——'

'I haven't been away long,' she interrupted, turning on Miles like a fury. 'It's useless trying to come the masterful bully with me, Miles Stanhope, because you're hopelessly miscast for the role. Besides, before I come for tea I'm determined to have a little flutter on the remaining races, since Ladies' Day at Ascot is likely to be a one-off in my life. Then—and only then—will I stay put in the box and act out your silly little charade to the bitter end. I simply *detest* all this stupid play-acting—I should never have listened to you in the first place.' Without waiting to see if he were following her Georgina stormed off to the nearest tote window, with Miles charging after her in hot pursuit, thoroughly alarmed by her outburst.

Miles failed utterly in his efforts to win Georgina round. The atmosphere between them was arctic as they returned to the box. Janus gave them a quizzical look as he handed round cups of tea, while Ros's greeting was so wistful that Georgina felt like a criminal as she tried to respond to Mr Stanhope's teasing about her beginner's luck. For the rest of the afternoon she remained at Henrietta Stanhope's side, with Miles dancing attendance on them both to such an extent that Georgina began to pray for it all to be over, her nerves stretched to breaking point by a combination of Rosalind's brave gaiety and the bright, challenging gaze Janus seemed to have trained on her own face every time she glanced in his direction. Her pleasure in the day evaporated so completely that it was even an effort to muster enthusiasm when her final three choices romped home easy winners.

It took some time for the Stanhope party to
return to the hired limousine, since Henrietta
Stanhope was, at last, beginning to flag. Georgina,
not liking the old lady's pallor at all, hurried ahead
with Miles and Rosalind to find the driver waiting
beside the Bentley, to their intense relief, as by this
time Janus was carrying his grandmother, Oliver
Stanhope hovering anxiously alongside, chafing his
mother's lax hand. Since Rosalind looked scared
to death, Georgina, calm despite her anxiety, soon
had Mrs Stanhope installed, half reclining, in the
back seat, a pillow beneath her head and her colour
slightly less ashen once Georgina had found her
heart pills and tucked one beneath her tongue.

'One thing's obvious,' said Janus tersely.
'Grandmother needs space for the journey home.
I'd better take someone in my car and come down
to Keyne Magna tonight, instead of returning to
town.'

'Well, it's not going to be Georgina,' snapped
Miles, dousing the flicker of hope in the bosom of
the lady in question.

Janus looked at his young brother with distaste.
'Don't be such an ass, Miles,' he said wearily. 'It's
only logical I take Rosalind so the Bentley needn't
make the detour through Naddersford.'

Rosalind, tearful and concerned, was plainly only
too ready to agree with whatever made it easier for
everyone, and went off meekly with Janus after
farewells had been made all round.

Georgina, once again racked with guilt pangs
over her false position, took one of the tip-up seats
alongside Miles, watching Mrs Stanhope anxiously
as the car joined the slow procession from the race-

course, relieved to see her revive considerably once the car was moving swiftly on the motorway. Even so, the journey back was very subdued.

'Don't fuss, children,' Mrs Stanhope commanded, and smiled at Miles's downcast face. 'Cheer up! I'm not about to turn my toes up just yet. For one thing, I'm determined to see you safely married, my boy, before I pop off.'

After which announcement Georgina sat in misery for the rest of the journey. It was an enormous relief to arrive at last at Glebe House, where Miles insisted on carrying his grandmother to her ground floor rooms, a very anxious Madge hard on his heels.

Oliver Stanhope took Georgina into his study. 'I should never have given in about this damned Ascot trip,' he said, looking desperately worried. 'But when my mother gets the bit between her teeth there's no stopping her.' He managed a smile. 'But how about you, m'dear? Did you enjoy your little flutter today?'

Georgina was able to say with complete truth that the whole day had been a truly unique experience. She thanked him, then excused herself to change for the drive home. Dressed in trousers and shirt, her finery packed away, she went down to find Miles, waiting for her in the hall.

'Let's go into the garden,' he said, looking oddly stern. 'I'd like a little chat before you take off.'

Conscious that Oliver Stanhope was watching them indulgently from the study Georgina went without argument in the direction of the walled garden, where, Miles said firmly, they could have a private talk without being overlooked from the house.

'How's your grandmother feeling now?' asked Georgina as she paced up and down with her restless companion, who had substituted jeans and sweat-shirt for his former sartorial glory.

'Much better. Madge says a good night's rest and she'll be as right as rain. The day was too much for her, that's all.'

'I can well believe it,' agreed Georgina heavily. 'It was too much for me too.' She took the ring off her finger and held it out to him. 'Here. I'm not wearing it another minute. The game's over, Miles. I won't play any more.'

Miles pocketed the ring then led her to a stone bench overlooking a herb bed. 'That's what I want to talk about.'

'There's nothing *to* talk about,' said Georgina impatiently. 'I shall leave in a minute, after which you can make a clean breast to your family about me, about Linda Potts, and anything else on your conscience, just so long as I'm well away out of it all. End of story.'

Miles turned to her, seizing her by the elbows. 'That's just it. I don't want it to be end of story, Gee.'

She stared at him in blankly. 'What are you on about, Miles?'

His fair, handsome face took on a stubborn look. 'I suppose it was seeing you with Janus. I'd never realised—I mean, you've always been just Harry's little sister. Then I saw him with his hands on you and I—well—I was bloody jealous.'

Georgina's eyes opened wide. '*Jealous!* You, Miles—of me?'

He nodded, his hands tightening on her arms. 'Forget about a pretend engagement, Gee, darling. I want it for real...' He frowned at the appalled look on her face. 'What's the matter?'

She sighed. 'Miles, you can't possibly mean what I think you mean.'

'Oh, yes, I do,' he declared and grabbed her into his arms. 'I really do fancy you.' And to prove his point he bent his head and kissed her for the first time in the seven years of their acquaintance. Georgina, too astounded to protest for a moment, never even heard the footfalls on the gravel path surrounding the vegetable plot until a cold, disdainful voice made her shove Miles away, her face burning with embarrassment as she jumped to her feet to see Janus, still in his Ascot finery, regarding them with distaste.

CHAPTER FOUR

'I ASSUME,' said Janus, his eyes icy with disapproval as they stared at Georgina's dishevelled curls, 'that Grandmother is better. Otherwise not even you, Miles, would be out here making love to Georgina.'

Miles rose to his feet, trying to look unconcerned. 'Gran's OK now, as a matter of fact. And whether I make love to Georgina is my business, Janus.'

'I would have thought it was Georgina's,' observed Janus, and turned on his heel to stride away in the direction of the house.

'You know,' remarked Miles, staring after him, 'I rather think my big brother fancies you too, Gee.'

Georgina felt fed up to the teeth by this time with both brothers. 'I really don't care whether he does or not,' she lied, suddenly at the end of her tether. 'And no more nonsense from you, either, Miles. I wouldn't marry you if you were the last man on earth.'

Miles glared at her, incensed. 'Why not?'

Georgina pushed a weary hand through her hair. 'All sorts of reasons. I'm fond enough of you, but not in that way. You've got a lot of growing up to do yet, Miles—and I've neither the time nor the inclination to help you do it. Go away and play with Linda Whatsit, or something—all this talk of marriage is just silly nonsense.'

Miles took a great deal of convincing that she meant what she said. He gazed at her with indignant blue eyes, and would have gone on arguing indefinitely if Georgina hadn't cut him off by announcing it was high time she left, and hauled Miles off to find his father so she could say goodbye.

'But, my dear, you must have a meal before you go,' said Oliver Stanhope kindly. 'Madge has something ready and waiting—you can't drive all that way without something to eat!'

Georgina assured him that she couldn't eat a thing after such a wonderful lunch, then sent her best wishes to Henrietta Stanhope, who was reported as sleeping peacefully, to Georgina's infinite relief. Miles, remarkably silent since the episode in the garden, opened the Mini's door for Georgina just as Janus emerged from the house dressed in a white polo shirt and faded old Levis, his hair wet from a hasty shower.

'Leaving so soon?' he asked, frowning.

'Persuade her to stay,' urged his father, but Janus shrugged indifferently.

'That's Miles's department—as he made very clear to me a short time ago.'

Oliver Stanhope looked from one son to the other in amusement, then kissed Georgina on the cheek. 'Thank you for coming today, my dear. It made an old lady very happy.' He pressed Georgina to come again soon, then signalled to Janus to accompany him inside the house. After a moment's hesitation, Janus, with no vestige of warmth in his manner towards her, said goodbye with formality to Georgina and left her alone with Miles, who immediately asked her to think again about his proposal, apparently still unable to believe he'd been turned down.

Georgina shook her head. 'Nothing doing, Miles. I meant every word.' A shiver ran through her at the very idea of becoming Janus Stanhope's sister-in-law. 'Now go in there and tell your family the truth about us,' she said relentlessly.

Miles winced. 'Look, Gee, couldn't we leave it for a bit till Gran's feeling more the thing? Then in a week or two I can just say we didn't hit it off, or something—unless you change your mind in the meantime.'

She sighed impatiently. 'No—I *won't* change my mind.' Then inspiration struck. 'In words of one syllable, Miles, I won't marry you because I happen to be in love with someone else.' And, leaving Miles standing deflated in front of his beautiful home, she drove carefully through the old iron gates and set off on her journey back to everyday life.

Georgina was glad of her everyday life over the next few days. A spate of weddings, parties and funerals proved very effective in taking her mind off Janus Stanhope, leaving her too weary to drive to Hereford to spend Sunday with her parents. She gave an account of her day at Ascot over the phone to her mother instead. Margaret Griffiths, expecting a euphoric description of it all, was plainly surprised at Georgina's reluctance to talk about anything other than seeing the royal family and her extraordinary luck with her gambling.

'Do I take it you're tired of playing games and pretending to be what you're not, Georgina?'

'Yes.'

'Does Miles know this?'

'Yes.'

'How about the rest of the family?'

'He asked to postpone telling them until his grandmother's completely well again—say it didn't work out for us, or something,' said Georgina moodily. 'I just wish I'd never got myself involved.'

'Do you, darling? Honestly?' Her mother sounded amused. 'If you hadn't you might never have met Janus Stanhope, remember!'

And probably would never hear from him again, thought Georgina, depressed, in which she was proved ecstatically wrong when, late on Sunday evening, he rang her up, saying 'Georgina?' in a caressing tone which raised every separate hair on her spine at the sound of it.

'Hello,' she said in a stifled voice. 'Who is this?'

'Janus Stanhope. How are you, Georgina? You know, you worried me the other night. You looked far too fragile to drive all that way after the alarums and excursions of the afternoon.'

Georgina, who was five feet eight inches tall, and generously curved, had never been called fragile in her life, and felt so flattered she could hardly speak. 'I—I look pale when I'm tired, that's all,' she said breathlessly.

'I know. I've already noticed how those freckles of yours darken like early warning signals.' His voice dropped half an octave, affecting Georgina's knees so badly that she slid to the floor in a heap.

'Your father rang me to say your grandmother's better,' she said, deciding to get off dangerous ground. 'I'm very glad.'

'So am I, and it was very thoughtful of you to write and send her flowers. Nevertheless, my grandmother is not the reason for my call, little one.'

Little one? thought Georgina, dazed.

'I'm ringing because I'm worried about you and Miles,' he went on.

'You needn't be,' she assured him.

'Frankly, until Thursday, I wasn't all that much. In fact I was sure young Miles was having us on about you, Georgina, to put us all off the scent about the delicious Linda Potts.'

Georgina bit her lip in guilty silence as Janus went on to tell her that it was the scene he'd interrupted in the kitchen garden which had shaken his theory.

'Was it love among the turnips after all, Georgina, or had Miles seen me coming and made damn sure I witnessed the kiss?'

'Miles was—was pressurising me into naming the day,' said Georgina with a rush, feeling this was a fair stab at the truth.

There was silence for a moment. 'And did you?' he asked at last.

'No.'

'Good. You're much too young.'

'If you say so.'

'I do. Or perhaps what I mean is that you're too young to marry Miles, who's a damn sight too immature to marry anyone.' He paused. 'If business matters bring me down your way again soon, will you let me take you out to dinner, Georgina?'

'No,' she said, quelling a strong desire to say yes. 'Under the circumstances I don't think it's ethical.'

'In that case I see I'll have to see what I can do to bring about a change in these circumstances of yours. Goodnight, little one.'

Janus rang her several times during the next couple of weeks, ostensibly just for a chat, yet each time he ended by repeating his invitation to dine, and each time, because Miles had asked her to wait until after his grandmother's birthday before he confessed, Georgina felt duty-bound to refuse. Not at all sure of Janus's motives for ringing her, she nevertheless looked forward eagerly to the phone calls, which were frequent enough to elevate her to a floating pink cloud of anticipation as the day of Mrs Stanhope's birthday grew closer.

How happy she would be when the embarrassing truth was known, thought Georgina, when Henrietta Stanhope rang with an invitation to her birthday lunch on the following Sunday.

'At my age each birthday is a triumph worthy of celebration,' she informed Georgina, chuckling. 'Do say you'll indulge an old woman's whim—not to mention make Miles happy—by coming to help blow out the candles.'

Miles was surprisingly apologetic when he rang Georgina about the birthday party. This time it was none of his doing, he assured her—in fact he was still smarting from Harry's trenchant instructions to leave his little sister out of any future harebrained schemes.

'Though why he keeps referring to you as little, I don't know,' said Miles tactlessly. 'You're as tall as I am.'

'What a silver-tongued devil you are, to be sure, Miles,' said Georgina crossly and put the receiver down with a bang.

It rained for the rest of the week, which cooled the atmosphere, but weighed down on Georgina's spirits. The weather meant fewer customers than usual in the actual shop, but otherwise the normal behind-the-scenes activity went on unabated, and, with the idea of looking her best for the occasion, a weary Georgina decided to get to bed very early on the eve of her last appearance in public as fiancée to Miles Stanhope.

When she arrived at Glebe House next day Georgina found the forecourt so crowded with cars she parked the Mini near the Old Forge Garage as before. She slung her bag over her shoulder, then picked up the gift she'd brought for Henrietta Stanhope and set off across the village green, her heart leaping to her throat as she saw Janus Stanhope emerge from the gates of Glebe House at a run to meet her.

'You're late!' he informed her, smiling as he relieved her of the large box. 'Where've you been?'

As he spoke the church clock chimed the quarter.

'Only fifteen minutes late,' said Georgina, so pleased to see him again her answering smile was incandescent. 'The motorway was crowded, and my car seemed a bit sluggish today. Hardly surprising—she's not exactly in her first youth.'

'Unlike her owner.' Janus paused, staying her with a hand on her elbow. His dark eyes studied her from head to foot, lingering longest on her smiling mouth. 'You look about sixteen in that pink dress, little one.'

'Whereas I'm almost five years more than that, but thank you for the compliment—if that's what it is.'

They stood looking at each other in silence, their smiles fading in unison as Janus leaned closer, taking her hand. His eyes narrowed as he looked down at her ringless fingers.

'What happened to the ring?' he asked.

'None of your damn business!' said Miles, dashing up to join them. 'I'll take Georgina in, if you don't mind.'

Janus looked dangerous for a moment, then shrugged. 'Temper, temper, infant. Perhaps it's time we all went in. Grandmother was beginning to worry about you, Georgina.'

The entire Stanhope clan was gathered together in the garden behind Glebe House, along with many of the people Georgina remembered seeing at the wedding, including the bride and groom, newly returned from their honeymoon. Georgina's welcome was warm. She was drawn in at once to the crowd gathered round Henrietta Stanhope, who sat enthroned in the midst of it, like a queen receiving her subjects. Her smile was mischievous as she eyed Georgina's brace of escorts.

'Ah, there you are, child. We were wondering if you'd changed your mind about coming.'

Georgina bent to kiss the soft, wrinkled cheek. 'Hello, Mrs Stanhope. Sorry I'm late—I'm a slow driver, I'm afraid.' She turned to take the large box Janus was carrying. 'Many happy returns. I hope you'll like this.'

Everyone gathered round to see the latest birthday tribute. As Janus removed string and paper

from the large carton Henrietta Stanhope waited
with anticipation, excited as a young girl, as a
bonsai tree was revealed in all its miniature perfection, planted in an exquisite porcelain bowl.

'My dear!' breathed the old lady in delight. 'How
extravagant, and how utterly lovely. I've always
yearned for one of these. How did you guess?'

'I hoped,' said Georgina, smiling happily at the
other woman's obvious pleasure.

'Clever girl! Miles, get your Georgina a drink at
once—oh, look, dear, there's your brother.'

Georgina gave a gasp of surprise as Harry de-
tached himself from a group of young people and
strolled across the lawn to give her a kiss, grinning
all over his face.

'Hello, Carrot-top. Didn't Miles say I was
coming?'

'Miles,' drawled Janus, 'can hardly be described
as the most efficient of fiancés.'

Harry looked surprised. 'But hasn't——?'

'Hello, brother dear,' said Georgina swiftly,
giving him a charged look. 'Nice surprise.' She
turned, smiling her thanks, as Miles dashed up with
a glass of Pimms.

'OK, Janus,' he said shortly. 'You're relieved of
duty now.'

Janus looked down on his younger brother for
a moment, his face set, then he turned to Georgina.
'Since you're in safe hands for the moment,' he
said, touching Harry's shoulder deliberately, 'I'll
circulate with the Pimms jug. See you later.'

'Do I detect a spot of fraternal discord?' enquired Harry.

'Just Janus doing his big brother act.' Miles scowled. 'Frankly, he dances a damn sight too much attendance on Georgina for my liking.'

'Don't talk rot, Miles,' said Harry briskly. 'You aren't really engaged, you idiot.'

'Not for want of trying,' retorted Miles. He eyed Georgina gloomily. 'I don't suppose you've changed your mind?'

'Absolutely not,' she assured him. 'I told you why.'

Miles appealed to Harry. 'She says she's in love with someone else. Anyone *you* know?'

Harry looked hard at his sister. 'No,' he said softly. 'I don't. Should I, pet?'

'No, you shouldn't,' said Georgina blandly, and handed him her glass. 'Here, drink this, there's a love. I can't cope with alcohol at this time of day.'

But Harry wasn't listening. He was gazing with appreciation at the two latecomers hurrying in to apologise to Henrietta Stanhope. One was Ros, looking flushed and pretty in a bright yellow dress. The woman with her was also dark, but several years older, in jade raw silk shirt and trousers tailored to hug every sleek curve.

'Who's *that*?' asked Harry, with a silent whistle.

Miles shrugged. 'Liza Verreker—and Ros, of course.'

'Haven't seen Ros for ages,' said Harry, and, with a word of apology to Georgina, made a beeline in the direction of the newcomers.

Georgina watched with amusement, as her brother attached himself to the two young women the moment they'd paid court to Henrietta Stanhope.

'Not surprised,' observed Miles. 'Liza's a knockout, isn't she? Ros's sister, you know. Broke every heart in the neighbourhood before she got married.'

Georgina eyed the striking brunette with interest. 'Is her husband here?'

'Which one?' Miles guffawed. 'She's had two to date, but got rid of both. Probably looking round for a third as we speak. Better warn Harry.'

Georgina chuckled. 'I don't think that's necessary, Miles. I rather fancy it's Ros he went dashing off to chat up.'

Miles looked at her askance. 'Ros? You must be joking!' He stared across the lawn at the animated group gathered round Liza Verreker, scowling as he realised Georgina was right. The others in the group were talking to Liza. But Harry's interest was quite plainly centred on a flushed, smiling Rosalind.

'Well, I'm damned!' said Miles, and took hold of Georgina's arm. 'Come on, Gee, let's break it up. Harry's a bit too high-powered for Ros.'

Georgina pulled away crossly. 'You go if you want. I'd like to tidy myself up a bit.'

'OK,' said Miles absently, and hurried off towards the others, leaving Georgina alone in the middle of the lawn for a moment before she turned on her heel and went in the house, making for an upstairs bathroom. When she emerged Janus was waiting for her on the landing.

'I saw,' he said grimly. 'Why the hell do you bother with him?'

Georgina shrugged. 'Sometimes I wonder! Is there anything I can do to help?'

He shook his head. 'Our wonderful Madge roped some people in from the village.' He took her by the hand, smiling down at her with a wicked glint in his eyes. 'Let's play truant.'

Janus took a swift look about him then led Georgina stealthily down the stairs and along the deserted hall towards the back of the house to his father's study. 'Madge would probably have a fit if she saw us here,' said Janus, ushering her inside. 'My father never lets anyone in to tidy it up.' He turned the key in the lock, then led her to the sofa, and Georgina, not at all sure she should be consenting to all this, sat down obediently on the rubbed velvet cushions of the sofa, feeling breathless as Janus let himself down beside her with a sigh, sliding his arm along the back so that it brushed her hair.

'You know perfectly well we shouldn't be here,' she told him severely. 'Not when your grandmother's birthday is going on outside—and certainly not with the door locked.'

'I don't want anyone barging in,' he said emphatically. 'Not now when I have you here in person, as it were.' He stroked her hair delicately. 'I'm tired of talking to a disembodied voice, little one. I just want a few minutes' conversation with a girl I can see, and touch.' He touched a fingertip very lightly to the freckles on her cheek. 'Not just any girl, of course. Only you, Georgina.'

She tensed at his touch, and he smiled faintly, an indulgent smile curving his mouth.

'Tell me what you've been doing since I last spoke to you,' he commanded.

'I've been working hard,' she said, staring down at her clasped hands. How ridiculous it was to feel so shy! She'd been alone with Janus before. But once he knew the truth she might never be again, she reminded herself. Not after today.

'So have I,' said Janus and reached a hand to turn her face towards him. 'So. Having disposed of our activities since we last met, what shall we talk about now?'

Georgina looked up into his eyes, abandoning all effort to conceal her fascination with this urbane, sophisticated man who seemed like the hero in every fairy-tale she'd ever read. 'To be honest I don't really think we should *be* talking——'

The rest of the sentence was lost instantly against his mouth, as, with an air of man tempted beyond reason, Janus kissed her in a way which made her senses reel. Her lips parted in rapturous response as her arms slid round his neck, and Janus held her so close she felt his heartbeat against her breasts as his mouth grew more and more urgent. She tore her mouth away at last, her eyes enormous in her parchment-pale face.

'I *meant*,' she said raggedly, 'that we should join the others.'

'I know, I know, little one. But I'm not made of stone. How could I resist?' Janus rang a long finger over her cheeks and across her mouth, lingering at the deep indentation of her upper lip for a moment before he bent to replace his finger with his mouth, and Georgina gave up, giving him back kiss for kiss, feeling him taut against her, his arms cruelly tight for a moment, before he drew away with a reluctance he made no attempt to hide.

'I told you before,' he said harshly, 'that if you were mine I'd lock you away rather than have you kiss another man like that. You remember?'

She nodded wordlessly.

'Do you love Miles?' he demanded.

Georgina swallowed.

He shook her gently. 'Aren't you sure, Georgina?'

Ask me again tomorrow, she thought in anguish, sorely tempted to tell him the truth there and then. But a promise was a promise, even to Miles.

Janus waited, his face dark and intent. 'Even if you do,' he said deliberately, 'I can change your mind.' And he slid his hands into her hair and kept her face immobile as he kissed her in a way which made nonsense of any resistance. And all this tumult, she recognised dimly, was merely her response to his kisses. Heaven help her if he...

Georgina pushed him away, trembling. 'We must go back to the party—we'll be missed.'

Janus took her hand and pulled her to her feet, then turned her so that she could see their reflections in the mirror over the fireplace. 'Look at yourself, darling,' he said, his breath warm against her ear.

Georgina looked, horrified, at her dishevelled hair and red, swollen mouth, at the freckles standing out in dark relief against her pallor.

'Glory, what a fright!'

'You're delectable,' he contradicted swiftly, and planted a kiss on her shoulder. 'Let's sneak out before the gong goes and I'll smuggle you upstairs before the others lay eyes on you.'

Like conspirators they crept hand in hand from the room, but no one was in sight. Janus gave her a little push across the hall and she flew upstairs, almost colliding with someone emerging from the bathroom.

'Oops, sorry,' said a husky voice. Two bright dark eyes viewed Georgina with interest. 'Hello. We haven't been introduced. I'm Liza Verreker, and you're Miles's Georgina.'

'How do you do?' Georgina managed a smile, grateful for deliverance as the gong sounded below. 'Must tidy myself up before lunch.'

'Sensible idea,' observed the other woman, eyeing Georgina's face.

She smiled and went on her way downstairs, leaving Georgina to shut herself in the bathroom with a moan of horror as the sunlight pouring through the window revealed the full picture of the havoc Janus's lovemaking had wreaked on her hair and face. Not one detail of which, she knew, had escaped the glamorous Mrs Verreker.

When Georgina went downstairs again the party was in full swing. A noisy throng filled the dining-room, busily providing themselves with delicacies to take outside to eat in the sunshine, and Henrietta Stanhope, installed at a small table at the end of the room, beckoned to Georgina.

'Come along, child. You must try some of this chicken dish of Madge's. It's her speciality. No need to stay here with me,' she added, as Georgina brought her laden plate and sat beside her. 'I can't take the sun very much any more, but you ought to be out there with the other youngsters. Why isn't Miles looking after you?'

'I'd rather sit here with you. Without a hat I'm hopeless in the sun, I'm afraid.' Georgina smiled as she gestured through the open windows at Miles, who was perched on a low stone wall with a crowd of others. 'Miles is out there with Harry.'

'He should be here with you,' said Henrietta Stanhope tartly. 'Where's Janus?'

Georgina busied herself with her meal. 'I think he's circulating with wine.'

She could see him outside, helping his father see that everyone's glass was filled, and after a while Georgina saw him jerk his head at Miles and say something, after which Miles, looking rather truculent, marched into the dining-room.

'Just came to see if you're OK, Gee,' he said virtuously, and began refilling his plate. 'Can I get you anything, ladies?'

'Perhaps you might ask Georgina what she'd like to drink,' said his grandmother, raising an eyebrow. 'You've been neglecting her.'

Miles had the grace to look ashamed. 'Sorry, Gee. What can I get you?'

Georgina accepted a glass of lemonade, then took pity on Miles and told him to go out into the garden again. 'I'd rather stay here, Miles. You go back to the others.'

'If I do I'll have Janus on my tail,' said Miles, and perched himself on a stool near his grandmother's feet to eat his second helping of lunch. 'He booted me in here so he could chat up Liza in my place.'

Georgina couldn't help a quick look out into the garden where, as Miles said, Janus was conducting a spirited exchange with the vivacious Mrs Verreker and her young sister.

'Perhaps he's seeing Rosalind is looked after,' said Henrietta Stanhope.

Miles frowned. 'I shouldn't think so. Ros is just a kid.'

'How old *is* she?' asked Georgina.

He shrugged. 'Not sure. Couple of years younger than me, I suppose.'

Henrietta Stanhope looked at Georgina. 'And just how old are *you*, my dear?'

'I shall be twenty-one in a month's time.' Georgina gave Miles an arctic little smile. 'Which makes me even more of a kid.'

'True,' he agreed, unmoved. 'Between you and Ros, Janus seems to have developed a taste for the nursery lately.'

Georgina bit back an angry reply, as the efficient Madge came in with her helpers to clear away the lunch, ready to serve the puddings.

Henrietta Stanhope smiled indulgently. 'Run away, Georgina. Go and find your brother, and some of the young ones. Your manners are a credit to your mother, but you don't need to stay with me all the time.'

'I enjoyed it,' Georgina assured her.

Miles took her by the arm and pulled her outside to return to the laughing group gathered round the newly-weds, who were telling tall tales about their honeymoon wanderings in Australia. Harry jumped up as Georgina approached, giving her his place, and Ros welcomed her warmly, drawing her into the conversation as Miles pushed himself into the space between Georgina and Liza Verreker, who was deep in low-toned conversation with Janus. He turned as he noticed the new arrival.

'Will you be all right in the sun, Georgina?' he asked, interrupting Liza mid-sentence.

'That's a point,' said Harry, and took a pair of dark glasses from his breast pocket. 'Here, put these on, Carrie. You should have brought a hat.'

'I'll get one of mother's,' said Janus swiftly, and went striding off across the lawn into the house.

'Dear me,' drawled Liza. 'Perhaps I should dye my hair red—seems infallible for attracting male attention.'

Ros frowned at her sister. 'Georgina's got delicate skin.'

'You'd think all those freckles would protect it from the sun.' Liza smiled lazily.

Georgina smiled back, ignoring a sudden impulse to scratch the heavily painted eyes out. 'I only wish they did. It must be marvellous to have oily skin like yours, Mrs Verreker.'

Harry trod on her toe and began an involved story about the time he and Miles got sunstroke bicycling in France, by which time Janus was back with a straw panama his grandmother used for gardening.

'Not in quite the same class as those Ascot butterflies of yours,' he commented with a smile. 'But at least you won't have a headache.' He turned to Miles. 'Right. Let's get some coffee for our guests.'

CHAPTER FIVE

GEORGINA found the rest of the afternoon trying. Miles took it in his head to resume his role of fiancé and stayed firmly beside her, blocking every move by Janus to usurp his place. She sat in silence for the most part, content to listen to the others, not fully recovered even yet from the illicit episode in the study. Janus stood nearby, his eyes straying to her averted face from time to time, and Georgina, aware of him in every fibre, moved closer to Harry, who peered questioningly under the brim of the panama, then slid his arm round her waist as he countered some quip from Miles.

Georgina avoided Janus's eye purposefully, and tried hard to keep her eyes off him altogether. Why, she thought, dazed, was he making such a dead set at her? Was his aim solely to detach her from Miles, or was he really the type of man who had to prove his machismo by annexing any feminine scalp which came to hand? It was just possible he really did feel something more—more significant as far as she was concerned, of course. She brightened. It would be very gratifying to think he was truly attracted to her. Perhaps a man like him, accustomed to sophisticated, experienced women in the circles he moved in, found the contrast of her own simplicity and inexperience refreshing. On the other hand, she thought wryly, for someone like herself to set out to bring a man like Janus Stanhope to heel was rather like taking on the role of lion tamer without any whip or chair for protection.

Georgina's reverie was interrupted by the sight of Madge wheeling a large birthday cake out on a trolley. There were loud cheers as Henrietta Stanhope made a gallant effort to blow out the candles, aided by Janus and Miles, who then conducted a spirited version of 'Happy Birthday' from everyone present. It was late in the afternoon before people began to drift away. Georgina began to think longingly of home. All this subterfuge was a draining sort of business. Janus or no Janus, she wanted to go. For a moment she was alone with Harry as Miles and Janus went off to speed parting guests.

'Is Miles telling his family it's all off tonight?' Harry demanded in an undertone.

'He'd better.' Georgina pulled a face. 'It's a ghastly strain pretending to be something one isn't.'

He eyed her searchingly. 'What was all that about being in love with someone else, by the way?'

'Something I made up to stop Miles talking rot about marrying me.'

He looked relieved. 'Good. For a moment I had the wild idea you might have meant Janus. Which wouldn't do at all.'

Georgina shrugged, feigning an indifference she didn't feel. 'Purely a hypothetical question, of course, but why not?'

Harry looked distinctly uncomfortable. 'Look, love, I like Janus. He's a great guy. But Casanova was a rank amateur compared with him when it comes to women. And it's common knowledge that the minute a girl looks like getting any ideas about wedding bells he takes off at a rate of knots.' He cleared his throat. 'What I'm trying to say is that compared to a chap like Janus Stanhope you're a babe in arms, Georgina.'

She winced. Harry only ever used her given name when he was in deadly earnest. 'All of which, I assure you, is totally irrelevant as far as I'm concerned. Don't worry, brother dear. Even a babe in arms like me sports the odd shred of common sense, you know.' She looked up and smiled as Miles rejoined them. 'Time I was off, Miles.'

'But Gran wants you to stay to supper. Harry, too,' he added.

'Not on, I'm afraid,' said Harry regretfully. 'Must be back in town by eight.'

'Meeting a girl?' asked Miles, brightening.

'No. Playing squash.' Harry grinned. 'Don't worry, chump. I was just being friendly with Ros.'

Miles stared at him, startled. 'What do you mean?'

Harry shook his head, grinning at Georgina. 'He doesn't even know, the fool.'

Georgina was fast losing patience with Miles. 'Look,' she said sharply, 'when are you telling your family about us?'

'Tomorrow,' he promised. 'Gran's had enough excitement for today. I swear I'll come clean tomorrow, honest injun.'

Georgina sighed. 'Oh, all right. But I'm not staying to supper, Miles. I'm tired.'

Harry kissed her, then went off to say his goodbyes, by which time only Ros and Liza were left, and Henrietta Stanhope insisted they all go in

the house and have a rest over more coffee before
the girls set off for home.

'You in particular, Georgina, with that tiring
journey ahead of you,' she said firmly. 'I know
there's no point in asking you to stay the night because you probably have to be up at the crack of
dawn tomorrow.'

'What *do* you do, Georgina?' asked Liza
Verreker.

'She runs her own florist's shop,' said Janus, beginning to hand round cups.

'Fancy,' said Liza in mock admiration as she
smiled up at Janus. 'A businesswoman, no less.'

'And so young,' put in Oliver Stanhope, smiling
at Georgina. 'Must have a good head on your
shoulders, my dear. Will you sell up when you
marry Miles?'

Georgina went cold. 'I—I hadn't thought that
far.' She gave a quick look at Miles, who flushed
and looked away, offering no assistance.

'Will the wedding be soon?' asked Liza, with a
sly look at Rosalind's downcast face.

'No,' said Georgina, swallowing her coffee as
quickly as she could, then got up. 'I really must
go. Thank you for a lovely party.'

It seemed a long time before she could extricate
herself from the round of thanks and good wishes.
Georgina came to Janus last, smiling steadily at him
as she held out her hand.

'Goodbye. It was nice to see you again.'

Janus's face was inscrutable as he shook her
hand, murmured something polite, then his grandmother brushed him aside to kiss Georgina and
press her to come to see them again soon, and Miles

was pulling her away and they were outside and on their way back to the Mini, and it was over. Miles chatted as they went but Georgina never heard a word. Was that it? *Was* it all over? Somehow she'd expected... What had she expected? That Janus would clutch her to his bosom, declaring she belonged to him, not Miles? She came to with a start, to see Miles staring at her strangely.

'Are you OK, Gee? Did you hear what I said?'

'No. Sorry. What was it?'

He looked offended. 'I was merely asking, and boring you to death by the look of it, whether you really meant there was no chance for us. For you and me, I mean.'

Georgina sighed wearily as she unlocked her car. 'Oh, Miles. Once and for all, no. It's plain as the nose on your face that you and Ros are meant for each other.'

He stared at her, open-mouthed.

'It's true,' she assured him. 'You should have seen your face when Harry was chatting her up. Like a puppy which has had its bone snatched away.' She turned the key in the ignition. Nothing happened.

'What is it?' asked Miles. 'Flat battery?'

'Can't be. I bought a new one a couple of weeks ago.'

'Come out. I'll have a try.'

It was no use. Nothing either of them tried brought the little car to life.

'Sorry, old thing,' said Miles, scratching his head. 'No use my tinkering with it—I'm useless with machinery.'

Georgina leaned against the little car with a sigh of despair. 'Is there a local taxi firm?'

'In Keyne Magna?' hooted Miles, then brightened. 'I'll get Janus to lend me his car. I'll drive you home.'

He dragged a protesting Georgina back to Glebe House, where her predicament was greeted with differing solutions. The older Stanhopes thought she should stay the night and get her car mended at the Old Forge Garage the following day. Miles brushed this aside, appealing to his brother hopefully.

'I thought you might lend me your car to drive Georgina back.'

Janus stared down at him in disbelief. 'You must be joking!' He turned to smile at Georgina, who by this time was wishing she'd never left home. 'Don't worry. *I'll* drive you.'

'And who,' murmured Liza, 'said chivalry was dead?'

Miles began to argue, protesting that it was his place to get Georgina home, and that all Janus had to do was trust him with his wretched car for a couple of hours.

'I wouldn't trust you with it for five minutes,' said Janus, already shrugging himself into his jacket. He patted Miles's head kindly. 'It isn't insured for you to drive, old son. And even if it were I've far too much civic conscience to let you loose on the public in it.'

Everyone laughed. Miles's lack of skill behind the wheel was renowned. Ros put a consoling hand on his arm as Georgina, very embarrassed about the whole thing, asked Oliver Stanhope if he would arrange a tow to the local garage in the morning, then made what she devoutly hoped was her final round of farewells.

Once outside Georgina forgot any awkwardness as Janus led her to the sleek red monster crouched on the gravel of the courtyard.

'Crikey!' she said inelegantly, as he helped her in. 'Did you rob a bank for this?'

Janus grinned, looking a lot happier than he'd done for hours. 'Certainly not. Can't bite the hand that feeds me. I work in a bank, remember.'

'So you do.' Georgina looked at him apologetically as the Alfa Romeo coupé roared to life. 'I'm so sorry about this. I'm being a dreadful nuisance.'

'No, you're not.' He said nothing for a moment or two as he drove through the gates and out on to the road. 'I'm very happy to take you home.'

'You'll be late getting back.'

'It's not important.'

'On the other hand, I quite see why you wouldn't let Miles let loose with a gorgeous car like this.'

'My dear child, even if it had been a beaten-up old banger I still wouldn't have let him have it. You don't seem to understand. I *want* to drive you home. I'm deeply grateful for a couple of hours alone with you, and not,' he added, with a swift sideways glance, 'so that I can make love to you again. I'd be lying if I said I don't want to, I confess, but I'll enjoy the drive and a talk almost as much, little one.'

Georgina, a prey to varying emotions in response to this, found her weariness had vanished completely, taking all the guilt and uneasiness of the day along with it as she relaxed, breathing in the expensive leather smell of the car interior.

'What happened to all the talk? You're a very silent companion,' he observed, once they were on the motorway.

'I was just enjoying the ride.' She chuckled as the car ate up the miles effortlessly. 'It's a lot different from my poor old Mini.'

'You need a new car.'

'Can't be done. The delivery van for the shop took all the spare cash.'

Janus touched a hand to hers as they lay clasped in her lap. 'What a responsible young lady you are, Miss Griffiths.'

'That's not the way I see myself,' she confessed. 'When I'm with you I feel young and gauche and horribly unsophisticated.'

'Then you hide it well, little one.'

'How can you say that after—after——'

'After the time we spent together in the study?'

'Exactly.'

Janus was quiet for a moment. 'That, really, was what I wanted to talk about.'

Georgina tensed. 'You don't have to. Really. I'm not that young. I mean I realise it was just—just an interlude. An accident, if you like.'

'On the contrary,' he said, a rather grim note in his voice. 'I took you in the study for the precise purpose of making love to you. To prove something to you.'

'Oh?' she countered coldly. 'And what was that?'

'I wanted to show you how wrong you are for Miles, and how right you are for me.' Janus said it so casually Georgina's eyes flew to his still profile in astonishment.

'What—what do you mean?' she asked carefully.

'I mean, dear child, that, regrettable though it may be, I covet my brother's future bride.' Janus caught one of her hands in his and raised it to his lips before releasing it. 'Give Miles up, Georgina. Now. Before things get too complicated all round. It shouldn't be too difficult—just a matter of exchanging one Stanhope for another, after all.'

Georgina felt winded. She stared blindly ahead of her as they drove at speed towards the setting sun, unable to take his words in.

'Well?' he prompted. 'Is it possible I was mistaken, after all? I could have sworn the feeling between us was mutual, right from that first moment in Chelsea.'

Georgina bit her lip in silence, very wary after Harry's little sermon. What, precisely, did Janus have in mind? Since he possessed a well-publicised aversion to marriage it seemed pretty certain he wanted them to become lovers. Not that she herself wanted marriage, by any means. She had no desire at all to give up the business she'd just established. But, because Janus's life was based in London, even a less permanent relationship presented problems. They were worlds apart in almost every way— except for a certain undeniable chemistry.

When Janus broke the silence he sounded strained. 'Do I take it that I *was* mistaken then, Georgina?'

'No,' she admitted honestly. 'You weren't mistaken at all. I felt the same the moment I saw you.'

He let out a deep breath. 'In spite of Miles?' he asked.

'Miles never came into it,' she assured him with complete honesty.

'Then give him up!'

'Yes. I will.'

Janus crushed her hand in his, then changed the subject very deliberately, leaving her all at sea as he questioned her about her friends and interests, then told her about a recent project he had been engaged in at his bank. Georgina talked and listened, half of her so happy she could hardly believe this was happening, the other half very apprehensive about several things, not least the thought of what Janus might expect to happen at journey's end.

Georgina felt sick with nerves by the time Janus slotted the Alfa Romeo into a corner of the deserted car park behind the shop. As he switched off the engine she looked up at him uncertainly.

'Are you coming in?'

'I hope so,' he said very softly, and raised her hand to his, pressing a kiss on the palm before sliding out of the car. He helped her out, looking over his treasured possession with great care before he locked it, then followed her through the alley which led directly from the car park to the goods entrance of the shop.

Georgina's fingers trembled as she unlocked the outer door. Janus took the key from her to lock it behind them before they climbed the stairs to her flat in a silence which grew unbearably tense as she ushered Janus into the flat. As she switched on the light he looked very tall and overpowering in her minuscule sitting-room, all at once so much the sophisticated stranger that Georgina quailed.

'Darling child,' he said swiftly, taking her hands. 'Don't look like that. My confession in the car doesn't mean I'm going to pounce on you, demanding instant access to your bed!'

Georgina, who had feared just that, relaxed, her smile rather rueful. 'Sorry! I'm not used to this sort of situation. Would you like some coffee?'

He laughed. 'Yes. Of course I would.'

'Only instant, I'm sorry,' she said as she filled the kettle behind the tiny counter which divided the kitchen area from the room.

'Instant's fine—stop apologising.'

'I'm nervous!'

'I know. But there's nothing to be nervous about, I promise.' Janus took the tray from her and set it down on the table, then drew Georgina down beside him on the cramped sofa, which, apart from a dilapidated armchair, was the only piece of furniture to justify the room's description.

'It's just that you're a man with a very different lifestyle from mine, Janus,' she said frankly. 'You look like someone used to fast cars and vintage wine, custom-made clothes, meals in expensive restaurants——'

'Hey!' Janus took her by the elbows and shook her a little. 'I work for a merchant bank, little one, not own it. Besides, even if I do like all those things, I like others, too. Just sitting here with you, for a start.'

'Why?' she asked baldly.

His eyes narrowed. He stroked her hair with a caressing hand, taking his time over answering. 'I thought I'd told you that,' he said at last.

Her eyes fell. 'I suppose I just find it hard to believe.'

'Now it's my turn to say why.'

'I didn't want to come to your sister's wedding, you know. It was a great effort to turn up alone. Then I saw you.'

Janus took her hand in his. 'And?' he prompted softly.

'I—I was struck dumb.' Georgina looked up at him suddenly. 'I couldn't believe I was actually face to face with the man I saw at the Chelsea Flower Show. It seemed like a dream. But I thought it would be like one of the crushes one gets in school. That once I didn't see you any more I'd get over it.'

'Like measles.' His eyes were bright with irony.

'No!' She gazed at him pleadingly. 'What I'm trying to say is that I never imagined for a moment you'd feel the same. We're so different, you and I——'

He frowned. 'Age, you mean?'

Georgina shook her head impatiently. 'No. What does that matter? I mean the things I listed just now. *They* make up the real contrast between your life and mine. My parents are the best in the world, but Dad's the accountant of a small manufacturing firm, and he lives with my mother in a nice modern house in a little close of a dozen others exactly like it. Whereas your home——'

Janus put a hand under her chin and brought her face up ruthlessly to his. 'Hey. Steady on. All this is completely irrelevant. For one thing Glebe House has never really *been* my home. My parents lived in Home Counties suburbia when I was young. Dad bought the place in Wiltshire ten years ago, not long before Mother died. These days we tend to tease him about his new country squire persona, but he worked damned hard in the City when he was young, made sure his sons received the best education possible, and now he's enjoying the fruits of his labours, unfortunately without my mother to share them.'

Georgina braced herself. 'I have to mention something else, too,' she said doggedly.

Janus put out a hand to raise her face to his. 'Go on.'

She met his intent eyes head on. 'At the risk of sounding stuffy, there's the small matter of your reputation with my sex.'

He stared at her in silence for some time. 'Will you believe me,' he said at last, 'if I say it's highly exaggerated? And even if I had played the field quite as much as reported, there comes a time in every man's life when he finally finds what he's been looking for all along.'

Georgina's mouth dried at the look in the eyes regarding her so steadily. She drew in a deep, quavering breath, the happiness flooding through her drowning any last lingering doubts and apprehensions.

Janus raised her hand to his lips. 'Is there anything else troubling you, darling?'

The endearment vanquished Georgina completely. She shook her head, unable to trust her voice.

'I suppose it was Miles who enlightened you about my past,' he said grimly.

'Not Miles—Harry,' she informed him apologetically.

'Ah!' He grimaced. 'I suppose I can hardly blame him. It's only natural for him to feel protective.'

Janus frowned suddenly. 'Why should Harry think I was any danger as far as you're concerned?'

Georgina's eyes fell. 'He saw us together today, I suppose.'

Janus smiled ruefully. 'You see? I'm not the expert you think I am when it comes to women, after all. I thought I was hiding my feelings very well.' He seized her hands. 'So. If I assure you that the past is the past, can we forget the other so-called differences between us? Harry's not bothered by those at least, so why should you be?'

'Harry's not in love with you!'

Janus gave a crow of laughter. 'Thank heavens for that.' He sobered, his eyes narrowing as they searched hers. 'Did you mean by that rather elliptical statement that you *are*, Georgina?'

She smiled suddenly, a radiant mischievous smile which made him catch his breath. 'You can't have been listening!'

He touched a finger to the indentation in her top lip. 'Not as attentively as I should, I confess, because I want like hell to kiss you.'

She dropped her eyes demurely. 'You may, if you wish.'

Janus got up and held out his arms. 'Come here, Georgina.'

She got to her feet, her eyes glinting green as she moved into his embrace. 'Why not on the sofa?'

'Because for the time being I think it best I stay on my feet when I make love to you.' He smiled down at her crookedly. 'It's not only safer that way, but you're tall enough to make it very easy to kiss you standing up. With shorter ladies one gets a crick in one's neck.'

'Does one, indeed?' Georgina aimed a little kick at his shin, then held up her mouth to be kissed.

Janus paused, a hair's breadth from her lips. 'If you keep injuring me like this I'll develop a permanent limp.'

'Sorry,' she whispered, gazing up into his eyes.

'How sorry?'

For answer she stood on tiptoe, wreathed her arms about his neck and kissed him full on his mouth. Her reward was instant. She felt the shock of response in Janus's body right through her own as he pulled her close, returning the kiss with a heat which bathed her entire body in an answering glow. Yet even as his kisses grew wilder and her responses more abandoned she sensed an iron restraint beneath his urgency, his arms remaining locked about her, with no move to caress her body or seduce her into anything more intimate in the way of contact.

When Georgina felt she could no longer breathe, that her body was like an unexploded bomb with the desire dammed up inside her, Janus stood back at last, his scar standing out lividly as he made a heroic effort to keep himself in check.

'Darling, I must go,' he said hoarsely.

She nodded dumbly, a glisten of tears in her eyes.

He snatched her into his arms. 'Don't cry, little one.'

'I'm not crying. And I'm not little. You said I was tall enough to kiss!'

He laughed unsteadily, burying his face in her tangled curls. 'The term "little one" is relative. I've never used it before. But then, I've never felt protective about a woman before. **When Miles left you** to fend for yourself today I wanted to knock the living daylights out of him, tell him he didn't deserve you. And he doesn't.' Janus drew back to look down into her rapt face, and shook her gently. 'I'm not setting foot outside this room until you tell me it's really over between you and Miles.'

'Oh, it is,' she assured him gladly. 'Utterly and completely.' She hesitated. 'In fact, Janus, I've got a confession——'

The telephone rang, interrupting her, and with a frustrated sigh Georgina went off to answer it. Janus followed her, his eyes never leaving her face as he leaned in the open doorway of her room.

'Hello, Miles,' she said, resigned, and Janus went to her swiftly, sliding his arms round her waist from behind.

'Is Janus there?' demanded Miles.

'Are you here?' mouthed Georgina, twisting her head round.

Janus nodded, grinning.

'Yes, Miles. He's just leaving.'

'Good. Gran wants to know if he's coming back here.'

'Are you driving back to Glebe House tonight?' asked Georgina in a voice made rather strained by the fact that Janus had his lips to the hollow behind her ear, sending hot and cold shivers up and down her spine.

'Yes. I'm setting off now,' he whispered, and Georgina duly relayed the message, said she'd be in the shop all day to receive news of her car, then put the phone down and twisted round in Janus's embrace, her mouth lifted eagerly to meet his.

It was a long, long time before they broke apart. When Janus touched a hand to her cheek Georgina was awed to find his fingers shaking as they stroked her skin.

'I'm going, Georgina,' he said huskily, 'before I yield to temptation and beg to stay.' He kissed the tip of her nose. 'I give you due notice, darling. Some day soon I'm going to achieve my heart's desire and kiss every single freckle, one by one. But for the moment I'm off. I'll ring you tomorrow. Goodnight, little one.'

He kept her close as they walked to the door, kissed her one more time, then put her away from him firmly, telling her to make sure she locked up securely before he disappeared into the darkness of the alleyway on his way to the car.

CHAPTER SIX

NEVER a fan of Mondays at the best of times, Georgina found the next day hard to live through. She was busy enough, as usual, but so keyed up at the prospect of Janus's call that the hours dragged interminably. Miles rang during the afternoon, sounding brusque and hostile, to say Georgina's Mini had needed only a very basic repair. He had, he announced grimly, a bone to pick with her after he'd driven the car down to her that evening, after which he would go on to London by train.

Since both Chris and Karen were in earshot Georgina was unable to do more than enquire guardedly whether Miles had done as she'd asked yet.

'Oh, yes,' he snapped. 'Janus saw to that.'

Which left Georgina in a state of unrest so total she found it hard to concentrate on the flower arrangements for a golden wedding celebration. Her nimble fingers were left to work independently of her brain as she automatically created exquisite confections of yellow roses and chrysanthemums, her mind occupied with Janus to the exclusion of all else.

Georgina was in the untidy, dank little room at the very back, clearing some of the litter of discarded greenery from the sinks, when Karen came through to say someone required Georgina's presence.

'Miles?' asked Georgina, resigned, as she dried her hands.

'Not unless Miles is dark and glamorous,' said Karen giggling.

Janus? Georgina flew to the front of the shop, forgetting her grubby green apron, then came to an abrupt halt, amazed to see Liza Verreker on the other side of the counter, looking like an illustration from Vogue, her expertly made-up face wreathed in smiles.

'Mrs Verreker? What a surprise. What on earth brings you here?'

Liza smiled lazily. 'Winning Brownie points, darling. I volunteered to chauffeur your car down here for you. Don't worry. I'm on my way to London. I can get a train here in half an hour.'

Georgina took off her apron, introduced her visitor to Chris and Karen, then asked the former to lock up for her while she took Liza Verreker upstairs to the flat.

'At least let me offer you a drink, or some tea.' She waved her unexpected visitor to a seat. 'Why didn't Miles bring the car back? He said he would.'

'Nothing, thanks.' Liza patted a voluptuous hip. 'Must watch the calories! Someone rang Miles up wanting him to dash off at once to take photographs in Bali, would you believe? Needless to say, he dashed! I happened to be at Glebe House collecting the scarf I left there yesterday, so I offered to drive your car down.' She held out the keys. 'I left it in the car park at the back here.'

'Why, thank you. It's extraordinarily kind of you.'

'Not in the least.' Liza opened her bag and took out a mirror to examine her face. 'Actually, I was rather glad of the chance to talk to you.'

Georgina balanced on the edge of the table, her long legs braced. 'Really?' She eyed the other woman uneasily.

'Yes.' Again the feline smile. 'I gather Janus succeeded, then.'

Georgina stiffened. 'Succeeded?'

'He's always been fond of Ros, you see.'

'I don't understand.'

Liza shook her head impatiently. 'You must know that my idiot of a sister is eating her heart out for Miles—heaven knows why, he's the most tiresome boy.'

Georgina inclined her head. 'I could hardly fail to know.'

'So, when Miles produced you instead of the rather common little creature the family thought he was mixed up with Ros was utterly heartbroken. Whereupon Janus sportingly took it upon himself to lure you away from his little brother and leave the field clear for her.' Liza met Georgina's startled eyes head on. 'He told me Ros had no need to fret; it wouldn't take long for him to put things right. And it didn't. I gather it was too easy for words to decide you in favour of the mature, successful brother instead of a struggling photographer like Miles.'

Georgina felt like death. 'You were there when he got back?' she asked very quietly.

'Oh, yes. Mrs Stanhope insisted Ros and I stay for supper. It was all quite riveting, darling—Miles and Janus would have hit seven bells out of each other if it hadn't been for Oliver.' Liza gave her a pitying smile. 'I've known Janus a long time, you see. He does rather tend to hanker for other men's property—in fact, he was responsible for the break-up of my first marriage. Unfortunately he has this fatal flaw. Once the other man's property becomes his he no longer finds it so desirable.' She got up and started for the door, then paused, searching through her handbag. 'I almost forgot. Here's a copy of the bill for the car, so you can see what was done to it.'

'Should I pay you?' asked Georgina with icy calm.

'Oh, no.' Liza smiled. 'Janus had the bill sent to him. He said to consider the account for the car— and everything else—settled.'

Long after the door had closed behind her the scent of Liza Verreker's perfume filled the air. Georgina flung open all the windows, then threw herself face down on the bed. Why had he *done* it? It had all been so unnecessary! Janus hadn't needed his formidable battery of weapons to defeat her. She had never been any danger to Ros, or Miles, or anyone else. And if Miles had only told the truth about the silly charade weeks ago none of it would have happened.

Not quite true, she told herself bitterly. She would still have fallen head over heels for Janus Stanhope. But if he'd known the truth he wouldn't have felt obliged to make love to her to lure her away from Miles. And after a time, without any fuel to feed it, her pitiful little crush would have died a perfectly natural death. She banged her fist on the bed impotently. How *could* he? Her fears about the

differences between them had been well founded.
She'd been too young and inexperienced to recognise such a smooth operator at work. Harry had
been right, too, when he'd told her she was no
match for Janus Stanhope. And at last Georgina
gave way to tears of sheer misery, sobbing her head
out alone on her bed.

When the phone rang the first time she let it ring.
But when it rang again soon afterwards Georgina
made herself pick up the receiver.

'Hello,' she said thickly.

'Georgina? Henrietta Stanhope.'

Georgina screwed her eyes up in horror.

'Georgina? Are you there?'

'Yes. I'm here.'

'I just want you to know that Miles has told us
all about the little masquerade, and you're not to
feel badly about it. We quite understand.'

Georgina wanted to howl again. 'I'm so sorry,
Mrs Stanhope,' she said brokenly. 'I never meant
to upset anyone.'

'Nor did you my dear. And now we know exactly
how things stand I want you to come and see me
as soon as possible, in your true colours as it were,
this time.'

Mrs Stanhope went on to ask if the car had arrived safely, to apologise for Miles in his absence,
and assured Georgina that she herself was in very
good shape after her party, then asked if Georgina
had a cold.

Georgina fibbed about a sore throat, then forced
herself to ask for Janus's address and phone
number. Mrs Stanhope, plainly surprised Georgina
didn't know it already, obligingly supplied the

necessary information before repeating her invitation, and sending best wishes from her son.

Afterwards Georgina sat on the edge of the bed, the piece of paper with the number on it clutched in her hand. What time did merchant bankers get back from their giddy round of wheeling and dealing? she wondered. She dialled the number with a trembling finger before she could change her mind, and at the first sound of Janus's voice her heart turned over. The deep, confident tones struck Georgina like a blow, so that it took her a moment to realise she was listening to a recorded message. She put the phone down, scribbled a few words on the message pad, struck some out, altered others, read them through again then dialled his number once more. She listened numbly to his recorded voice then at the sound of the tone said her piece, her voice so thick with tears it was barely recognisable.

'This is Georgina Griffiths. I've put a cheque in the post for the car repair. Congratulations on winning your wager so easily. I regret you were put to so much unnecessary trouble.'

Having started she longed to say more, but the answering machine cut her off. She contented herself with making out the necessary cheque, then put it in an envelope, ready to post in the morning. Then she looked up the name Janus in her encyclopaedic dictionary. The Roman god Janus, she learned, her lip curling, was always depicted with two heads facing opposite ways, his name a byword for hypocrisy.

Georgina was in the bath when the phone rang again. She lay there, her fingers in her ears, until it stopped. But a few minutes later it rang again, and she wavered. It might be her mother. She bit her lip. She couldn't take the chance. It probably wasn't Janus, anyway. But it just might be. Once the phone stopped again she dialled her parents' number quickly, learned her mother hadn't phoned that evening, had a short chat, then took the jack from the socket and lay back on the bed, limp with relief. Now she was safe.

For the first day or two Georgina felt she'd hit on a good idea. Her personal telephone was merely an extension of the one in the shop below and could be disconnected each evening. She rang her parents before leaving the shop each day, then spent the evenings with only the television, her books, and the disconnected telephone for company. Unfortunately she could do nothing about the telephone in the shop below, which was faintly audible no matter how high the volume of her radio or television. Convinced every time that it must be Janus, she stalked about the flat like a prowling lioness, ready to scream by the time it stopped, exerting every ounce of self-control she possessed not to connect her own extension and scream at him to leave her alone. Yet at the same time she was irrational enough to indulge in daydreams about Janus tearing down from London in his Alfa Romeo, demanding to see her, saying it was all a big misunderstanding. When he did no such thing the last of Georgina's illusions died a sad little death, and she started on a determined effort to forget she'd ever laid eyes on Janus Stanhope.

Her recovery plan suffered a set-back when Chris answered the phone in the shop one afternoon, shot a questioning look at Georgina, and scribbled on a pad, 'Janus Stanhope—yes or no?' Georgina shook her head wildly and fled to the scullery at the back out of temptation's way. Chris, after a wary look at Georgina's face later, asked whether she should give the same answer if the same gentleman rang again, and to her everlasting credit asked no questions, even when Janus rang twice more. By the end of the week there were purple shadows under Georgina's eyes, her nerves were in ribbons and she felt so utterly miserable that she escaped to Hereford for a weekend of tender loving care from her mother, putting off her return until the crack of Monday's dawn.

After her weekend break Georgina both felt and looked a lot better, to her colleagues' relief, until halfway through the morning when one of the receptionists from the Unicorn came in to order some flower arrangements for a Rotary dinner that evening.

'Tell Georgina we had that friend of hers in over the weekend,' she said to Karen.

Georgina left her task to stand at the top of the steps leading down into the shop. 'What friend is that, Sheila?'

'You know. The tall dark one you were in the bar with one night,' said Sheila, winking. 'You can't have forgotten. He's scrumptious.'

'Oh, that one,' said Georgina carelessly, limp with shock. 'I've been away. How long was he here?'

'Came Saturday evening. I'm not sure when he left. When can I have these?' asked the girl.

'Karen will pop them down after lunch,' said Georgina, resisting the urge to seize the girl and wring every last bit of information about Janus out of her by brute force.

Georgina, after a little lecture from her mother on the subject of facing up to her problems like an adult, obediently left her telephone connected when she went upstairs to her flat that evening, and was, inevitably, in the bath when it rang. She heaved herself out of the water, swathing herself hurriedly in a towel on her way into the bedroom to answer it.

'Well, well,' said the familiar voice bitterly. 'At last. Miss Georgina Griffiths, I presume.'

'Who is this?'

'Don't be silly,' Janus snapped. 'You know bloody well who it is.'

Georgina clenched her teeth as she yanked at her slipping towel.

'Are you still there?' he barked in her ear.

'Yes,' she said coldly. 'What do you want?'

'I want to talk to you—and don't hang up. I'm tired of playing games. But then, you like games, little girl, don't you?'

Janus, thought Georgina with some surprise, was hopping mad, by the sound of him. What right had he to be angry? *She* was the injured party.

'I have no idea what you mean,' she said with dignity.

He gave an ugly laugh. 'If you'll just do me the favour of listening for a moment or two I'll tell you exactly what I mean.'

'Sorry,' said Georgina shortly. 'I have nothing to say to you, and there's absolutely nothing I want you to say to me. Goodbye.' She banged the receiver down, plucked the jack from its socket with a silent apology to her mother, then turned up her radio full blast to drown out the telephone she heard ringing almost at once in the shop down below.

When it stopped Georgina ran more hot water into her bath, feeling angry and upset. It had not been a good idea to talk to Janus. Just the sound of his voice had shaken her badly. She should have slammed the phone down on him. But no! She had had to prove to herself that the sound of his voice would have no effect. And what a failure that had been. Just to hear him, angry and accusing, had brought to painful life all those feelings she'd been trying to stamp out.

Too restless to lie in the bath after all, Georgina stood up in the tub and turned on the shower, letting cool water stream over her head. After a while she felt calmer, but depressed. She rubbed listlessly at her hair then swathed it in a dry towel, wrapped herself in a bathsheet and went to fill the kettle. As she spooned instant coffee into a mug, a loud banging started up on the service entrance door downstairs in the alley, startling her badly. Surely someone wasn't trying to break in in broad daylight! She pulled herself together, cursing Janus for making her so jumpy. It was probably just Chris without her key, wanting something she'd left behind. Georgina pulled on a towelling dressing gown, thrust her feet into mules and hurried downstairs to the side door.

'Is that you, Chris?' she called.

'No, it's not,' came the answer. 'It's Janus Stanhope. Let me in.'

Georgina's jaw dropped. 'But I've just been talking to you on the phone.'

'The phone in my room at the Unicorn,' he informed her. 'And, since you refuse to answer yours, I'm here in person and here I intend to stay until you open the door.'

'I'll call the police,' she said instantly.

'Oh, I shouldn't do that, Georgina! Think of your customers. It might even get in the papers. Pretty local florist in row with London businessman. Police called in——'

Georgina slammed back all three bolts on the door, one after another, like pistol shots. 'All right,' she said coldly as Janus Stanhope pushed past her. 'You win. Say your piece—fast—then go.' Her mouth tightened as he looked very pointedly on the length of leg exposed by her brief wrap.

'I see you're expecting company,' he observed. 'I won't take up much of your time. But if we're likely to be interrupted by this Chris you're expecting, wouldn't it be better if you were wearing a little more?'

Not for the first time Georgina gave thanks for the gift of a complexion which hid the heat rushing all over her at the insult implicit in his tone. What a fool she'd been to imagine herself in love with this intimidating stranger. Even more of a fool, she thought derisively, to imagine he was in love with her.

'Very well,' she said brusquely. 'I suppose you'd better come up. But please don't be long.'

Janus's mouth twisted. 'You're too kind. What I have to say won't take long, you have my word.'

His word! thought Georgina. She went upstairs, furious that he was afforded such an uninterrupted view of her legs as he followed her up the stairs. She ushered Janus into her sitting-room with cold formality.

'If you'll take a seat for a moment, I'll dress,' she said and marched into her bedroom, slamming the door shut. She leaned against it for a moment, taking in several deep, deliberate breaths before she tore off the dressing gown and pulled on the first clothes which came to hand, careless of how she looked as she dragged a brush through her damp hair, which stood away from her scalp like electric wires as she wielded her brush with a force which hurt. Arrayed in an old navy guernsey of Harry's and a pair of faded denims, she thrust her feet into tattered espadrilles and went out to face the enemy.

'May I offer you a drink?' she asked perfunctorily, as Janus turned from moody contemplation of the street below.

'I haven't come here for a drink.'

They stared at each other, Georgina, as she well knew from her mirror, white as a sheet with her freckles in bold relief, Janus almost as pale beneath his tan, his scar standing out in a way she remembered far too well.

'What *have* you come for?' she demanded.

Janus passed a hand over his face. 'Now that I'm here,' he said tonelessly, 'I'm not sure.' His snort of laughter was mirthless.

Georgina shrugged, feeling rather better. 'Do please make your speech. Since you've come so far out of your way it seems a pity not to have your say.'

'May I sit down?'

'Of course.'

Georgina took the armchair while he let himself down with a sigh on the sofa.

He stared at her broodingly. 'I wonder why I ever imagined you were young and vulnerable.'

'I'm only a week or so older than when we last met.'

'I congratulate you. *I* feel I've aged ten years at least since that happy day.'

Her eyes glittered coldly as she waited for him to go on.

'I'm thirty-five years old, you know,' he said confidentially, 'and not since I was twenty has a woman ever taken me in as completely as you did.'

Georgina's chin lifted. 'It was no intention of *mine* to deceive anyone.'

Janus leaned forward as though someone had pushed him from behind. 'Then why did you let me believe you were going to marry Miles, lead me on to make such an utter fool of myself by——?' He paused at the sudden fury on her face.

'By seducing me away from Miles just to prove to yourself you could do it, you mean!' She shook back her hair angrily. 'I gather you're fond of doing that.'

Janus's eyes slitted dangerously. 'What the hell do you mean?'

'I heard it's the way you get your kicks—coveting your neighbour's wife and all that. Only in this instance it was your brother's fiancée.'

'I haven't a clue what you're getting at, except that you were not my brother's fiancée at all—nor ever intended to be!' He glared at her with hostility.

'Did you have fun, Georgina, playing your little games with me?'

'I did nothing of the kind,' she retorted angrily. 'I admit I was idiot enough to agree to come to the wedding as Miles's fiancée—and regretted it bitterly ever since. But when I gave in to Miles I genuinely thought it would be just for the one day.'

'Ah! But when your line hooked me in as well, you decided it would be fun to continue with it— to make an utter fool of me.' Janus leapt to his feet and went to stare out of the window, his hands in his pockets.

Georgina stared balefully at his back. 'You must be joking! I never imagined for an instant that a man like you, with a track record like Warren Beatty's, was indulging in anything other than a— a flirtation of some sort.'

Janus's laugh raised the hair at the back of Georgina's neck. 'A flirtation of some sort! Is that what it was?'

Georgina frowned. 'I'm curious to know the truth. What exactly happened when you went back to Keyne Magna that night?'

Janus turned to face her, a grim set to his mouth. 'Which night, Georgina?'

'You know perfectly well!'

'Not at all. If I've learnt nothing else, I realise one needs clarification where you're concerned, little girl. I want everything in words of one syllable.'

'Very well,' said Georgina levelly. 'As you know perfectly well, I'm talking about the day of your grandmother's birthday, when you so kindly drove me back home because I had problems with my car.

When you left you went back to Keyne Magna, where, I was told, there was some kind of scene.'

'I don't know what the hell Miles told you——'

'*Miles* didn't tell me anything. I haven't seen him since I left your house.'

'You mean to say he didn't even have the courtesy to ring you before he took off?'

'He may have done. I haven't been answering my telephone.'

'Don't I know it!' Janus returned to the sofa and sat down. 'All right, Georgina, if your ego wants it all, blow by blow, I drove like the wind that night to tell Miles you had no intention of marrying him. To my surprise he was highly amused. At first. Right up until I told him about my own intentions towards you. Whereupon he let fly with his fists.' Janus shrugged. 'I couldn't let him, of course, because he's nowhere up to my weight. Not that I wouldn't have relished giving him the hiding of his life, I admit, but my father came tearing out into the garden to separate us, wanting to know what the hell was going on, so I marched Miles into the house and made him tell the truth.'

'I hope someone made you do the same!'

Janus eyed her malevolently. '*I* had no need to say anything, Georgina. Miles was the one who'd been playing games. Besides, no one was interested in me at that point. My little brother was so furious he came out with everything he'd been storing up for years—the family's refusal to take his photography seriously, the pressure exerted on him to go into banking like me, their disapproval of some of his friends, especially Linda Potts, and finally, as his *pièce de résistance*, his resentment over the

constant matchmaking as far as Ros is concerned.'
Janus shook his head, the corners of his mouth
turning down. 'The poor girl went a ghastly colour
at that bit, yet my grandmother, far from having
a heart attack at the fuss, seemed actually impressed by Miles's outburst.'

Georgina felt a rush of compassion for the girl
forced to listen to it all. 'It seems to me Ros was
the one hurt most. She must have been utterly
humiliated. Particularly if Miles was cruel enough
to say I was roped in as protection against her.'

'Of course he did. Miles, as you know, is no re-
specter of feelings.' Janus grimaced. 'At which
point Ros decided enough was enough and stormed
off, dragging an unwilling Liza with her.'

'Bully for Ros,' applauded Georgina. 'Heavens,
what a fool I was to let Miles persuade me to come
to the wedding in the first place—or anywhere else.'
She pushed her hair away from her face wearily.
'Then you'd have been saved all the trouble you
took over stealing what you fondly imagined to be
your brother's property.'

'Trouble! You've been nothing but trouble to me
from the moment I first saw you,' he said harshly.

Georgina shrugged. 'Not according to Mrs
Verreker.'

He looked blank. 'Liza? What has she to do with
anything?'

'Ask *her*!'

Janus's face darkened with such hostility that the
atmosphere in the room fairly vibrated with it. 'I'm
asking *you*.'

Georgina complied hurriedly. 'She told me you
had a sort of bet with her that taking me away from

Miles would be no *trouble* at all. Absolute child's play. Which it was, of course.' She felt a rush of pleasure as her taunt scored such a palpable hit that his scar sprang into prominence against the dark colour flaring a danger signal along his cheekbones.

'Are you telling me you actually believed I would discuss you with Liza—*or* with anyone else?' He got to his feet, menace in every line of him as he glared down at her.

'Why not? After all, the lady came a long way out of her way to give me the glad news.' Georgina's eyes clashed defiantly with his. 'Besides, it all fitted so exactly. I never did find it easy to believe that someone like you could really be interested in a small-town girl like me. But the best bit,' she added, lip curling, 'was when she told me you were the reason why her first marriage broke up, not to mention your habit of losing interest in a woman once you've had the sport of taking her away from another man.'

Janus went livid with rage. 'This is supposed to be a habit of mine?'

'I've no idea. I'm merely telling you what Mrs Verreker told me.'

Janus turned away to the window, to stare sightlessly at the street below. 'Liza,' he said after a time, 'is indulging in a little character assassination at my expense. Probably because when we were young—even younger than you are now—we went around together for a few weeks one summer. Then I went up to Cambridge and as far as I was concerned it was over. Liza was furious over what she was pleased to think of as my desertion, and married someone else in a fit of pique. Not surprisingly, the marriage broke up within months. So in the loosest possible terms I suppose you *could* say I had something to do with the break-up of Liza's first marriage.' He turned to look Georgina in the eye. 'Whether you believe me or not is your choice, of course, but I swear I have never discussed you with Liza Verreker or anyone else until that night when I told Miles I wanted you for myself.'

'Wanted', thought Georgina bleakly. Wanted for what, precisely?

Janus bent to raise her chin with an ungentle finger, staring hard into her startled eyes.

'Well?' he demanded. 'Do you believe I'm telling the truth?'

She looked at him thoughtfully for a while. 'Yes. I do.'

'Why?'

'Because it would be so simple to disprove if you weren't, I suppose.'

He dropped his hand, his face set in harsh lines. 'I see. How foolish of me to expect simple trust.' His smile flayed her. 'And how much time and trouble we could both have been saved if only you'd answered your phone sooner. All this could have come out in the open long since.'

'Does it matter?' she said wearily.

He shrugged. 'It does to me. I couldn't come chasing down here after you before, because I've been abroad on business. I've telephoned you in vain from as far as France and Italy, you may like to know.' His mouth took on a sardonic twist. 'You know, I really believed I was past the stage of making such a fool of myself over a woman.'

Georgina rose to her feet, looking at him uncertainly. 'You came down here just to see me?'

'No, Georgina. Let us by all means deal in the honest truth. I did have business in Gloucester, but I used it as an excuse to stay down here over the weekend.' His mouth tightened. 'I was determined to see you somehow. Unfortunately my delectable quarry eluded me. Until now.'

Georgina backed away, suddenly panicking at the look in his eyes, but he leapt after her and seized her in his arms, holding her cruelly close, one hand wound in her hair to hold her still as he kissed her. After the first moment of shock Georgina fought like a wild thing to be free, but Janus held her fast, his breathing quickening, her writhings plainly adding to his pleasure in subduing her.

He raised his head a fraction to stare down into her incensed eyes. 'I thought I could go without this. But I can't.' His mouth twisted in a sudden, frightening smile. 'Don't be afraid. I won't hurt you.'

The blank glitter in his eyes frightened Georgina far more than his anger. She began to fight in bitter earnest. But Janus Stanhope was a tall, muscular man temporarily at the mercy of his own senses. He held her in a relentless grip, kissing her in such a bruising, punitive way that she was terrified.

'Please,' she choked, when she could. 'Don't be like this——'

But his only response was to stop her protest with his mouth, and Georgina shook with rage, cursing herself for her stupidity in ever letting Janus through her door in the first place. Then the pressure of his mouth altered subtly, masterfully persuasive now, and she shook even more, but for a different reason, as one of his hands slid beneath her sweater, the other splayed, long-fingered, at the back of her waist as he pulled her hard against him. Georgina's knees buckled, her hands clutched at his shoulders to steady herself, her mouth opened beneath his, desperate for air, only to receive his tongue instead. Their ragged breathing intermingled as his searching hand came up against a thin barrier of lace and he hooked his fingers between her breasts and and tore it impatiently away, but the sudden pain as the metal catch grazed her skin brought Georgina to her senses. She summoned up every shred of strength she possessed and tore herself from his grasp, dodging behind the sofa like a frightened child.

'Get out!' she spat, her eyes enormous in her paper-white face.

They stared at each other like enemies, the tension vibrating between them like a living thing, then Janus made an oddly defeated gesture.

'Don't worry, I'm going,' he said wearily, his pallor almost a match for hers beneath his tan. 'You can come out from there. I shan't touch you again.'

'You bet you won't!' She glared at him, her teeth sunk in her bottom lip to hide its trembling.

Remorse dawned in his eyes, as the full realisation of the fright he'd given her finally struck him. 'Georgina——' he began huskily, and started towards her, then stopped in his tracks as she cowered away. 'Don't—please! I can't stand to see you flinch away like that. I won't hurt you.'

'You said that before,' she reminded him, teeth chattering, then, as reaction set in, Georgina, much to her own disgust, began to cry. Tears rolled down her cheeks, and she turned away, mortified, sniffing hard as she rubbed her eyes.

'Georgina.' Janus walked very slowly towards her. 'Little one—please! Don't! I feel like a murderer.'

At the desperation in his voice Georgina cried even harder, and Janus gave a groan of despair. Handling her like a piece of priceless porcelain, he drew her from her retreat and took her gingerly in his arms, and, instead of cringing away, as he plainly expected, Georgina collapsed against him, burrowing her face into his shoulder, heedless of the tension in his body as Janus held her close.

'Georgina,' he said gently, and breathed in sharply as she pushed herself closer. 'For pity's sake, little one—I'm not made of stone.'

Her head snapped back, her reddened eyes met the look in his and abruptly all her fear and misery vanished as she stood very still within an embrace she realised Janus was fighting to keep impersonal.

'Don't look at me like that!' he said hoarsely, pushing her away. 'I'd better get out of here.'

'Please don't—not yet,' she heard herself saying.

'If I don't——' He stopped, clenching his teeth, his eyes closed.

'Yes?' she prompted. 'If you don't?'

'If I don't,' he said, looking at her with unmistakable meaning, 'I shall probably frighten you again. I'll be honest, Georgina—I'm all at sea with someone like you. The women I'm used to know the rules.'

'What rules?'

'Exactly! You're such a contradiction in terms, Georgina. One minute you're a mature young woman, the next a frightened child—one with no idea of her own powers of attraction.'

Georgina smiled up at him triumphantly. 'Are *you* attracted to me, Janus?'

He stepped back, looking stern. 'Stop playing games, Georgina. Surely you've learned your lesson by now.'

'I just want to apologise, that's all.'

Janus sat, half braced against the edge of the table, his legs slightly apart. 'And just exactly what are you apologising for?' he asked with irony.

Georgina looked at him in appeal. 'For deceiving you at first—though I'd never met you when I let Miles bully me into coming to the wedding. I was sorry I'd agreed once I *had* met you.'

'You mean this scarred face of mine gave you the horrors when I met you in the porch!'

'Quite the reverse!' She reached out a hand and touched the scar. 'It's very romantic. Makes you look like one of those duelling Prussians.'

Janus pulled a face. 'Not a bit of it. Someone's boot mistook me for the ball at school, that's all.'

'Oh, bad luck!' Georgina grinned, and suddenly the tension between them lessened. 'What I began to say was that——' She stopped, her cheeks suddenly warm.

'Go on,' he encouraged.

'No. I don't think I will.' She pushed self-consciously at her hair. 'I rather fancy I might be breaking one of those rules of yours if I did.'

Janus regarded her in thoughtful silence for a moment. 'Shall I tell you what *I* thought when we met that day?'

'Yes, please.'

'I took one look into your eyes and thought fate had been kind to me.' The corners of his mouth went down. 'Then Miles came out to claim you and I felt cheated.' His eyes held hers. 'From the minute I laid eyes on you I was determined to cut Miles out, you know.'

'Because of Ros?'

He looked blank. 'Ros? I never gave her a thought. I was struck all of a heap at the sight of *you*. For one thing I was sure we'd met before. And because I knew Miles was making a fool of himself over a model I suppose I'd been expecting some anorexic creature, all eyes and cheekbones. Whereas you didn't look like any model I'd ever met.'

'Very true,' said Georgina with feeling, and gestured down at herself. 'I'm a few sizes too big, for a start.' She regretted the gesture instantly, since it drew attention to that part of herself no longer confined by its usual undergarment. Harry's sweater was one from his youth, and small enough to cling rather too faithfully to the curves beneath it. Heat surged behind her concealing creamy pallor. She backed away, feeling breathless and idiotically shy. Janus reached out a hand to stay her, and slowly, gently, he drew her towards him until she stood between his outstretched legs, his hands clasped loosely about her waist.

'Look at me, Georgina,' he said softly, and she obeyed reluctantly, afraid of what she might see in his eyes. Her heart stood still as she found Janus looking down at her with a smiling cajolery rather reminiscent of Miles. 'I want very badly to kiss you again. Will I frighten you if I do?' he said very quietly, and she shook her head dumbly.

Very gently Janus drew her to him, but as his lips met hers Georgina's arms slid round his neck of their own volition, her mouth opening to his, and without warning fire raged in both of them, devastating and sudden, fuelled by the see-saw of emotions they'd been riding ever since his arrival.

His lips moved hungrily over her face, tracing her eyelids, her nose, her cheekbones, before being drawn back to the magnet of her mouth. Georgina trembled, her entire body alive with responses heightened by the stress of the past hour as she gave him back kiss for kiss. Her head went back in unconcealed rapture as he kissed her throat and in a sudden fever of impatience Georgina pulled away and dragged the sweater over her head, her face defiant and half fearful as she faced him.

'Georgina!' he said hoarsely, his eyes dilating as they rested on the opulent curves displayed to him with such erotic, innocent invitation he pulled her to him, his face buried in her hair as he caressed her urgently. 'You don't know what you're doing to me!' he said, demented.

Georgina's answer was to nudge her cheek against his until their mouths met again, and her hands were pushing at his jacket and undoing his tie, and he was helping her until he was stripped to the waist and she was crushed against him, and any rules Janus had ever played to were abandoned. Hardly knowing how they got there they found themselves in the bedroom, shedding their clothes in feverish haste as their mutual passion raged out of control, until Janus drew her down on the bed and into his arms and the first head to toe contact of a man's naked aroused body against her own brought Georgina to the full realisation of what she was doing. She gave a frantic gasp, then began to fight, in a desperate, undignified struggle to escape the enormity of what was happening to her, screaming at him to let her go.

Abruptly it was all over. Janus heaved himself up, rolling away to sit up with his head in his hands, while Georgina, trembling from head to foot, scrambled away to the other side of the bed, curling herself into a ball with her back to him as she hugged the quilt around her for protection.

CHAPTER SEVEN

GEORGINA buried her head deep in her pillow, trying to isolate herself from various sounds which told her Janus was resuming his clothes even faster than he'd thrown them off.

At the touch of his hand on her shoulder she shied away, eyes tightly closed until she heard the door close behind him as he left the room. She lay for a long time until at last she slid off the bed and wrapped herself in her winter dressing-gown, which was a relic of her schooldays, grey wool, felted with age, and about as unbecoming a garment as a dressing-gown was possible to be.

Georgina looked at herself in the mirror, surprised to find she looked very little different from usual, except for a slightly swollen mouth and a couple of tell-tale reddened patches where Janus's chin had made its mark. She met her eyes in the mirror. What did one do now in this sort of situation? In books when people made love they smoked cigarettes afterwards, or had a chat, or simply went to sleep. But she hadn't really made love with Janus. It had been more like war at the end. And he was probably horribly angry and perfectly entitled to be, what was more. She stood, irresolute, wondering if he was still out there in her sitting-room. She listened. There wasn't a sound. Her shoulders sagged. He couldn't have left, of course, because she had to lock the outer door behind him. She made a dispirited attempt to tidy her hair then braced herself and went out into the other room. Janus stood at the window, fully dressed and irritatingly immaculate, waiting for her.

'It was my fault,' blurted Georgina. 'I'm sorry. I'm to blame for—for leading you on.'

Janus's eyes shut tightly for a moment, then his lids flew open to reveal such a bleak expression that Georgina shivered.

'Of course you're not to blame, child,' he said wearily. 'I must have been mad to let things get out of hand like that. I'm deeply sorry.'

She bit her lip. 'It's those rules of yours. I broke them.'

Janus rubbed an unsteady hand over his face. 'You didn't even know what the rules were, Georgina.'

'I'd never let any man get as far as my bed before, you see.'

'Yes, I do see. Because it's now blindingly clear that it was that particular untouched air about you that attracted me in the first place!' His mouth twisted. 'Never having encountered it before in someone I was attracted to, I didn't even recognise it. What a prize idiot I've been, one way and another—comes of playing out of my league, I suppose.'

'You're angry.'

Janus eyed her without pleasure. 'You're right. I am.'

'I don't blame you.'

'With myself rather than you, Georgina, for letting myself get involved with you in the first place.'

'Because I won't make love with you?'

'No, blast it. Because you, quite obviously, have very little experience in these matters, and as far as you're concerned I have a damn sight too much. If you'll take my advice you'll look around for someone more suitable for your first sexual encounter. Preferably,' he added bitterly, 'a lover who doesn't make you scream with fright.'

'That's not fair,' she said hotly. 'What happened was an accident. And when I make love for the first time I don't want anything accidental about it. I want it to be with a man who tells me how much he loves me, that he wants me to belong to him forever. And I don't care a damn how naïve that sounds. Why else do you think I've reached my age still—still the way I am?'

'I see.' said Janus, without inflection. 'If, then, I had laid heart and hand at your feet before we reached your bed you wouldn't have screamed?'

Georgina shrugged. 'Since the question's academic you'll never know, will you?'

They looked at each other for a long moment, then Janus reached into his pocket for his wallet. He took out a cheque and waved it at her. 'I didn't cash this, by the way. Your recorded message was so unintelligible, one way and another, that I couldn't make out what it was for.'

'The bill for the car. The message Liza gave me was to the effect that you considered the account for that, and everything else, settled.'

Janus cursed softly. 'Liza seems to have been excessively busy on my behalf! I had no idea she still carried such a grudge against me. I left Keyne Magna first thing that Monday, Georgina, before your car was even towed away to the garage. My father must have paid the bill.'

Georgina gazed at him, biting her lip. 'Are you sure?'

'No. All I'm sure is that *I* didn't pay the damned thing.' Janus looked at his watch. 'I'd better go.' He handed the cheque back to her. 'That's it, then. No loose ends.'

Was this how it was to finish? thought Georgina, stricken. Did he really intend to walk out of her door and never see her again? 'Won't you have something to eat before you go?' she blurted, suddenly desperate to delay him.

He gave a derisive bark of laughter. 'After tying me up in knots with sheer bloody frustration you surely don't expect me to sit down to a meal and talk polite nothings!'

It was Georgina's turn to be angry. 'I was just being polite. Please don't let me keep you. I'm sorry I've caused you so much trouble—one way and another.'

'So am I.' Janus walked to the door, hesitated, then turned to look back at her. 'Before I go, shall I tell you what really needles me, Georgina?'

'By all means.'

'When you were pretending to be Miles's property, couldn't you have let me in on the secret? Surely you must have known I wouldn't give the game away! Couldn't you have trusted me?'

'I promised Miles,' she said woodenly, then her eyes fell away from his. 'Besides, I thought once you knew I wasn't really his fiancée you'd have no reason to—to be interested in me.'

Janus came back to stand in front of her, jerking her face up to his with an ungentle finger. 'You believed Liza, then, that I'm only turned on by other men's property?'

Georgina stared at him defensively. 'No. I hadn't even met her then. I just couldn't believe that a man like you, sophisticated, experienced, was attracted to a girl like me just for myself.'

'Ah!' He released her so suddenly she rocked on her heels. 'I can hardly blame you. I couldn't believe it myself when I learned how young you were. Which didn't stop me chasing you like a lovesick schoolboy, driving up and down that bloody motorway like a maniac.' His laugh was chilling. 'But no more, Georgina Griffiths. A man can only take so much. Tonight I've learned my lesson. The gap between us is nothing to do with background, or age, you know. It's a personality clash—and a great yawning chasm from where I stand.'

'I see.' Georgina held out her hand with cold formality. 'Then it's goodbye. Such a pity I didn't realise you expected to share my bed on such short acquaintance. I could have saved you a lot of wasted time and effort.'

Janus ignored the outstretched hand. 'You're wrong,' he said bitingly. 'If I just wanted "bed" as you put it, there are several available to me far more conveniently placed than yours.'

Georgina dropped her hand before she was tempted to hit him with it. 'Yes, of course. There must be. How very silly of me.'

The set look to his mouth softened slightly. 'Just to put things straight,' he said, rather as though he were discussing the weather, 'I never had any intention of taking you to bed, you know. What happened tonight was, just as you said, a complete accident.' His eyes narrowed suddenly. 'Although, as it turns out, it's a bloody good thing matters never did progress to their natural conclusion.'

'I'm in full agreement of course, but why, exactly?'

He shrugged. 'I would probably have been so thunderstruck to find I was your first lover I might have been moved to some archaic impulse of chivalry—even to offer my hand and so on.'

Georgina's widened scornfully. 'You've got to be joking!'

'Not entirely. Such rash acts of passion have a nasty habit of leading to unwelcome consequences.' One of his black brows rose in question. 'Unless of course you were armed against such an eventuality?'

Georgina stared at him blankly for a moment, then her eyes flashed. 'No,' she snapped, hanging on to her temper with difficulty as his meaning dawned on her. 'Since I'm not in the habit of opening my bed to the public it isn't something I've ever considered necessary.'

'The local male populace must be a very restrained body of men!'

'No more than anywhere else. I'm choosy about the company I keep, that's all.' Burningly angry by this time, Georgina flung back her head to glare at him. 'At least,' she added bitingly, 'I always have been—until now.'

Janus paled, throwing up his hand like a fencer. '*Touché*! My cue, I think, to relieve you of my presence.'

Georgina nodded brusquely. 'I'd be grateful if you would. Goodbye, Janus. I'll see you out.'

He stood looking at her for a moment, his eyes remote and impersonal, as though he'd decided to distance himself from the entire situation. 'It would have been far easier if Miles *had* brought his Linda Potts to the wedding. Then I'd never have met you, Georgina, and the even tenor of my life—and yours—could have continued, undisturbed.' He held out his hand with daunting formality. 'Goodnight.'

Reluctantly she put her hand in his, making the unwelcome discovery that in spite of everything his touch still had the power to affect her strongly, and what was more, Janus was aware of it, his eyes bright with mockery as he pulled her suddenly into his arms.

'To quote the bard,' he whispered against her mouth, 'just one last time, "come kiss me, sweet and twenty, youth's a stuff will not endure"—or something like that.'

Georgina made a stifled little protest, but his lips silenced it with what was meant to be a swift kiss, but which grew so heated and prolonged they were both shaken and speechless as he finally tore himself away.

'By the way,' he said hoarsely, after a taut, charged silence, 'who *is* the man you were expecting? This Chris of yours?'

Sorely tempted to lie, Georgina folded her arms across her chest to hide the tumult inside it. 'He's a she,' she admitted unwillingly. 'The lady who answers the phone to you when I won't. Chris is my partner in the business.'

'I see.' Janus waited for a moment, but when it became obvious Georgina had no intention of saying another word he he gave her an oddly formal little bow then turned away and went swiftly from the room, not waiting for her to follow as he ran down the stairs and out into the night.

And out of my life, thought Georgina bleakly as she locked the alley door behind him.

Hoping against hope that she would hear from him, despite their quarrel, Georgina's mood deteriorated as the days went by with no word from Janus. Disappointment warred with a great many other emotions as she spent each endless summer evening cooped up in the flat rather than risk missing the expected phone call. She was, she told herself, being very silly. Janus had made it pretty plain he didn't want to be bothered with her again. Screeching at a man like a banshee in the heat of that never-to-be-forgotten moment was more than enough to alienate any red-blooded male. She could hardly blame Janus for being angry. Yet the thought of never seeing him again drove her crazy with longing for the sound of his voice, let alone the sight of him, to the point where she cursed herself for being such a fool that fateful Monday evening. It wasn't even as though she hadn't wanted him to make love to her, she realised with painful insight. It had been a simple matter of principle.

Matters were made much worse by the fact that Georgina was by no means short of phone calls from other people. She rushed to answer each one in a fever of anticipation, her disappointment tearing her apart every time when none of the calls was from Janus. She even heard from Miles at last, who phoned to deliver heated reproaches on her turncoat preference for his brother, and to make an appeal to her as regards Harry's attentions to Ros. In Miles's opinion Harry was just trifling with Rosalind, and, he declared piously, he had no desire to see her hurt.

Georgina hooted in derision. 'You should have thought of that before,' she said witheringly, 'when you inveigled me into posing as your fiancée for starters!' She banged the phone down, fuming, and went to bed in a thoroughly bad mood.

'You look ghastly,' Karen told her one morning. 'Are you all right, boss?'

'I'm fine! Why wouldn't I be all right?' flared Georgina, then met Chris's startled eyes, and bit her lip, ashamed. 'Sorry. Got out of bed the wrong side.'

Karen patted her shoulder soothingly. 'Never mind. I'll make you some nice strong coffee, shall I?'

When Karen was out of earshot Chris raised her eyebrows. 'A man, I assume. The one you won't talk to on the phone?'

Georgina smiled sheepishly. 'Yes. Only I will talk to him now—if he should ring.'

'Ah!' Chris grinned, and didn't say another word, even when the expected phone call never happened.

Georgina's parents expressed concern in no uncertain terms at the sight of their weary, unhappy daughter when she arrived for the weekend, and asked anxious questions on the state of her health, her business and her life in general. Georgina did

her best to reassure them, but the moment Philip
Griffiths left his womenfolk alone together
Margaret Griffiths came straight to the point.

'Now tell me what's wrong. The truth, please,
darling.'

'I suppose you could say I'm suffering from heart
trouble. And it hurts,' Georgina added, trying to
grin. 'My little deception did me a whole lot of no
good, didn't it? I should never have let Miles con
me into going to that wedding. Then I'd never have
met Janus Stanhope again and I'd never have
learned what misery was actually like...'

Whereupon she dissolved into tears and sub-
mitted to a comforting maternal cuddle as she
poured out the whole story except for the episode
in her bedroom, which was something she felt
unable to talk about even to her mother. Especially
to her mother, she realised with a shudder.

The sensible advice she was given was to take up
squash again and go out with as many of her old
friends who asked, and generally to throw herself
into as much activity as possible in an effort to get
over her heartbreak.

'Because get over it you will, my love, in time.
Always supposing the gentleman in question allows
you to by keeping out of your life, of course,' said
Mrs Griffiths, smoothing back the tumbled red
curls.

'Oh, he won't bother with me any more,' said
Georgina bitterly. 'He made it pretty plain that I'm
much too immature and naïve for him. Ironic, isn't
it, since Janus Stanhope is everything I've ever
wanted in a man? And now I've met him no other
man in the world will ever do, damn him!'

* * *

A couple of evenings later Georgina had just got in from the squash club, feeling exhausted and hopeful of a good night's sleep for a change, when Harry rang.

'Mother says you're down in the dumps, Carrie,' he said without preamble.

'Did she say why?'

'I gather your love-life is giving you problems—don't worry, I wasn't given the gory details. I just thought you might like to come up here next weekend. I'll buy you a nice dinner at Harveys or Langans, or somewhere, to cheer you up.'

Georgina's eyes lit up for a moment, then she sobered. 'I'd come like a shot if it weren't for your fellow tenant, but I'm not sure I wouldn't murder Miles in my present mood.'

But Miles, it seemed, was off a day or two later to the United States with Oliver Stanhope on a holiday which incorporated a few days' work in Florida for a nature magazine.

'Tim and Julian will be here, of course, but you won't mind them—though I hope your embargo on Miles doesn't extend to sleeping in his bed.'

'As long as he's not in it, no! Thanks, Harry, I'd love to come.'

The prospect of a weekend in London helped Georgina enormously through the following week, bringing back a little of her usual sparkle, to her colleagues' relief. They refrained heroically from asking questions, and plied her with cream buns during coffee breaks instead, in an effort to offset Georgina's startlingly rapid weight loss.

'You look a bit peaky!' said Harry, when he met her off the train.

Georgina agreed cheerfully as she surrendered her suitcase to him for the short walk from Paddington to his flat in Bayswater. 'Off my feed a bit, that's all.'

'In which case, Carrie, it's a good thing the programme's changed for tonight.'

'You mean you're too broke to buy me dinner!'

Harry grinned. 'Not far off the mark, to be honest, but not the reason. We decided you'd prefer a party tonight instead.'

'We?' said Georgina suspiciously.

'Tim, Julian and me. Don't worry. Miles is winging his way to the Big Apple as we speak. So relax, my child. You won't have any hassle from that quarter tonight!'

Tim Webster and Julian Soames, former rowing blues for their college, and still enthusiastic oarsmen, were both over six and a half feet tall and of Herculean stature. They met Georgina at the door with open arms, swinging her from one to the other with such enthusiasm that she begged for mercy.

'You don't know your own strength, you gorillas,' she said, laughing. 'Nice to see you.'

They made it flatteringly plain that they were even more pleased to see her, leering at her in a highly gratifying way as they urged her to don her glad rags at top speed because their guests would be arriving any minute.

'Why didn't you come sooner?' demanded Tim, who was fair and bronzed and unfailingly amiable.

'Had to close my shop before I could come, of course,' Georgina retorted.

'Gorgeous, nubile, and you own property and earn money!' said Julian, who was still at law school. 'Marry me at *once*, you wonderful creature.'

'Pack it in, you clowns,' said Harry, and pushed his sister through Miles's door. 'I'll throw a pizza in the microwave while you get ready—and don't be long.'

'Could I have a shower instead of a pizza?' she bargained. 'I ate on the train.'

Harry looked sceptical about the latter, but decided against offering any argument, telling her she had twenty minutes maximum to get ready, including her shower.

Spurred on by jeers about any woman getting ready for anything in a mere fifteen minutes, Georgina bet them anything they liked she could do it, requested a polythene bag to keep her hair dry, and got to work.

Normally not given to green as much as redheads tended to be, Georgina had popped into the cheap and cheerful little dress shop near her own at lunchtime to buy a grass-green outfit in cotton jersey with a skirt both shorter and tighter than anything she'd dared before, and a loose, hip-length top with a low, square neck. She buckled a wide black belt over the latter round her newly diminished waistline, slid her feet into black linen pumps, then brushed her hair from root to tip until it stood out in a wild aureole round her head and shoulders, tying back a tress behind one ear with a black velvet bow. She added a pair of swinging silver earrings studded with green stones, a few quick strokes with a mascara brush, a smudge of shadow on her lids, then, just as the stereo in the communal living-room erupted into life, she outlined her mouth with a bright lipstick just in time to beat the deadline.

'Time up!' yelled one of the men, and Georgina emerged from the room, smiling triumphantly.

'Right. I won my bet. What do I get?'

'First taste of this concoction we've made,' said Harry grinning at her, while the other two reeled, hands over their eyes, mock-dazzled at the sight of her.

Georgina knew it was all a big con to cheer her up, but played along with gusto, realising she felt in better spirits than any time since the night she'd last seen Janus as she took a glass of the virulent-looking punch Harry was stirring in a mixing bowl.

'Crikey,' she gasped after the first mouthful. 'I thought I'd won the bet, not lost it!'

The party was a cheerful, noisy affair, with an astonishing number of people packed into the flat, every guest arriving with a bottle to contribute to the proceedings. Although a lot younger than most of the guests, Georgina was accepted into their midst at once, laughing and joking as she circulated with dishes of nuts and potato chips, before being whisked off to dance with Tim and Julian and a gratifying number of other young men who seemed only too eager to get to know Harry's little sister. After the occupants of the other flats in the house came to join in the fun, the music got louder and the noise a few decibels higher. Julian, who was an amazingly good dancer for someone of his height and build, seized on Georgina at the sound of his favourite record, bawling to everyone to clear a space as he proceeded to fling his helplessly laughing partner around in a *pas de deux* which owed nothing at all to classical ballet as they danced like maniacs together to the beat of Prince's '1999'. To crown the performance, Julian lifted Georgina right off her feet, twirling her round effortlessly to the imminent danger of everyone in the vicinity as the record came to an end.

Back on her feet, dizzy and exhausted, Georgina leaned against Julian, trying to get her breath back, until she realised Harry was talking to someone whose dark curly head, while not on a level with Tim and Julian, was nevertheless elevated enough above most of the crowd for Georgina to recognise Janus with a feeling of shock which hit her like a blow to the stomach. Although he was talking to Harry, his eyes were fixed on Georgina's face, the distaste in them unmistakable even across the crowded room as he took in her dishevelled appearance. She straightened, detaching herself from Julian, who grinned, asked if she was all right, then went on chatting up the girl next to him as Georgina wriggled her way through the noisy crowd, making for Miles's bedroom as fast as she could to hide herself away from the cynical dark eyes which had plainly not been at all impressed by her frenetic dance routine.

What on earth was Janus doing here? she thought, anguished, as she shut the door behind her, particularly since he'd had to arrive at the one moment of the evening when she was making a complete fool of herself. He'd looked at her just now as if she were some spoiled child, showing off in front of the grown-ups. She'd have something to say to Harry too, she thought, eyes kindling. What did he think he was playing at, inviting Janus

Stanhope to this sort of affair? Unless, of course he had no idea Janus was the man causing her heart so much pain and trouble.

The self-same heart gave a sudden, sickening thump in response to a loud knock on the door, then resumed its normal beat as Georgina realised it was Harry's voice outside in the hall.

'Carrie, are you in there? Can I come in for a minute?'

Georgina flung open the door, then stood still at the sight of Janus behind her brother, her bright smile fading abruptly.

Harry looked apologetic. 'Miles asked Janus to pick up the photographs he took of Katie's wedding. They're in his shirt drawer.'

'Hello, Georgina,' said Janus quietly. 'Are you well?'

'Yes. Very.' She smiled coolly and opened the door wider. 'Feel free to rummage where you want. I was just on my way back to the others.'

Janus caught her arm as she brushed past. 'Could I have a word with you?' He smiled at Harry. 'Perhaps Georgina can help me find these photographs while you get back to your guests.'

Harry looked at them both in turn, eyes narrowed. 'Don't be long then, Carrie,' he warned. 'The party's for your benefit, remember.' With a raised eyebrow which told Georgina very plainly her brother was now fully aware of certain facts she'd omitted to tell him, Harry returned to the fray, leaving an awkward silence behind him.

'I'm afraid I can't be of much use,' said Georgina at last, restive under the bright black gaze trained on her. 'I've never been in Miles's room before today. I don't know where he keeps his shirts—or anything else.'

'I'm sorry now I ever said I'd collect the blasted photographs.' Janus leaned one shoulder against the wall, hands in the pockets of his fawn cord trousers. 'I'm lunching in Keyne Magna tomorrow so my grandmother asked me to pick them up. If I'd known Harry was having a party tonight I'd have steered clear.'

Georgina glanced longingly down the hall towards the sounds of music and laughter. 'Not your sort of affair, I imagine.'

'By which, little one, I gather you consider me too much of a killjoy to enjoy what's going on in there.' The gleam in the dark eyes was sardonic.

Georgina, her heart thumping at the endearment, shrugged indifferently. 'Not at all. It's just that last time we met I seem to remember some talk about chasms and so on between people like you and me.'

'Seeing you here tonight rather proves my point.' He looked down at her legs. 'By the way, aren't you rather asking for trouble in that frighteningly short skirt?'

Georgina's eyes flashed dangerously. 'You don't like it?'

'I didn't say I didn't like it,' he retorted drily. 'Merely that I disapprove.'

'I'm afraid your approval—or lack of it—wasn't something I took into account when I chose this particular outfit, you know. Besides,' she added, her eyes clashing with his, 'even with more of my legs on view than usual I'm hardly likely to come to harm with *Harry* on hand.'

'In other words what you choose to wear is no business of mine.'

'Exactly, Janus. I couldn't have put it better myself.'

They stood eyeing each other with open animosity, until a burst of deafening noise blasted them as the door to the living-room opened and a stream of people went dashing into the kitchen, roaring with laughter, and Tim, following hard behind, caught sight of Georgina and came loping down the hall, grinning.

'Now then, sweetheart, can't have you lurking in dark corners with unknown gents——' The identity of her companion penetrated his bonhomie, and he came to mock attention, saluting solemnly. 'Oops, sorry, Janus. Didn't see Georgina was in such safe hands!' And he wheeled away, shouting, 'Hey, you lot, stop nicking the gin!'

'Nice to know I'm held in such respect!' said Janus drily. 'Time I went, I think, before I put a complete damper on the proceedings.'

'Do give my regards to your grandmother,' said Georgina brightly. 'I hope she's well.'

'Rather better than you, I fancy,' said Janus moving closer as a different record on the stereo made conversation difficult, even out in the hall. 'Have you been ill, Georgina?'

'Certainly not,' she snapped. 'I'm always pale. You've obviously forgotten.'

'No. I haven't,' he said without inflection. 'Neither your complexion nor anything else about you. More's the pity.'

They looked at each other without speaking for a long, tense interval, while the music throbbed against a background of laughter and loud, animated voices, then Janus's mouth twisted in a bleak, humourless smile which chilled Georgina to the bone.

'I must let you get back to all the jollity, mustn't I? Funny, really. I'd actually made up my mind to get in touch with you again, you know, to find out if this gap between us couldn't be bridged in some way. But seeing you tonight among that lot in there put everything into quite brutal perspective once and for all.'

Georgina's head went up proudly. 'You mean you discovered just how immature and silly I could be when I really tried? Even more so than last time we met, if that's possible.'

'Oh, no, Georgina. Thoughts of that occasion still keep me awake at night. Tonight it was the revelation of seeing you laughing and having fun with Harry's crowd.' The dark eyes glittered sardonically. 'The scales, as they say, fell away from my eyes rather dramatically.'

'In other words,' she said tartly, 'nothing's changed. You're you and I'm me, and never the twain shall meet.'

'Something like that.' Janus sounded mortifyingly bored. 'This now established beyond all doubt, my child, I think I'll take myself off— possibly even to find more congenial feminine company. I own to a need for a certain type of consolation.'

Georgina went rigid with outrage. 'Please don't let *me* keep you——' She broke off as Harry came towards them looking distinctly annoyed.

'You two still out here? Did you find the photographs, Janus?'

'Afraid I haven't even looked yet, old chap,' said Janus blandly. 'I was just enjoying a chat with your sister.'

'Time you got back to the others, Georgina,' said Harry firmly. 'I'll give Janus a hand.'

Georgina nodded obediently. 'Right. Nice to see you again,' she added casually to Janus, pinning a bright smile on her face as she marched down the hall to rejoin the party, all her pleasure in the evening utterly ruined.

CHAPTER EIGHT

MONDAY was an interminable day, getting off to a bad start when Karen breezed into the shop first thing agog for details of Harry's party, took one look at Georgina's face and dropped the subject like a hot potato. From then on both she and Chris kept so firmly to neutral subjects all day that Georgina hardly knew whether to feel glad or sorry when it was time to lock up and retreat to her flat. She was, she realised glumly, fast growing tired of the same four walls. Her flat seemed far too much like a cage of late, with herself like a restless lioness penned up in it.

Margaret Griffiths rang the moment Georgina unlocked her door, eager to hear about the party. The account her daughter gave was glowing enough, but strictly edited, with no mention of Janus, and nothing at all about Harry's subsequent lectures, which had been of the 'I told you so' variety, followed by strict instructions to his sister to stop playing with fire. The moment Mrs Griffiths rang off Chris phoned to say she'd left her shopping behind and would be grateful if her perishables could be stowed in the fridge, by which time Georgina was beginning to fancy something to eat for the first time all day, and was subsequently not at her most amiable when the phone rang yet again the moment she'd begun scrambling some eggs.

'At last,' said Janus. 'You *are* a popular lady.'

Georgina, attacked by a sudden rush of heat from head to toe at the sound of his voice, resisted the temptation to ask who was speaking, in case Janus accused her of being childish.

'Hello, Janus. I didn't expect to hear from you again.'

'No. I don't suppose you did. Don't worry. I'm not ringing on my own behalf.'

Georgina's eyes flashed coldly. 'I see.'

There was a pause. 'I'm ringing,' he said carefully, 'because there are some photographs of you among the ones I collected on Saturday night. My grandmother thought you might like to have them.'

'I would, very much. How sweet of her. Thank her for me.'

'I'll send them on, then.'

'Thank you.'

'My pleasure.'

He sounded different, thought Georgina. 'Are you alone?' she asked.

'No. I'm still in my office.'

'I'm sorry you were put to the trouble of ringing me.'

'Not at all.'

Georgina eyed the receiver malevolently, then to her horror said the last thing she had any intention of saying. 'Were you successful in finding the feminine consolation you were desperate for the other night?' she blurted, and cursed herself the moment the words were out of her mouth.

'Yes. I was.' His voice roughened suddenly. 'Why, Georgina? Do you care? Don't worry,' he added caustically, 'You can speak freely. I'm alone now.'

'You make your secretary work long hours!'

'She left some time ago. It was one of the cleaners.'

'Oh.'

'Why? Surely you're not jealous!'

'I may be young, Janus, but I'm not completely stupid.'

'I never thought you were,' he said caustically. 'I'm the stupid one for ever imagining a relationship between us was remotely feasible.'

'Something you changed your mind about the moment I wouldn't—wouldn't sleep with you, I suppose.'

'If that's what you wish to believe, Georgina, you are, of course, entitled to your opinion.' There was a long, tense pause, as though he was waiting for her to say something. 'I'll send on the photographs,' he said at last, chillingly distant. 'Goodnight.'

Georgina couldn't trust her voice to reply, and stood with tears sliding down her face, still as a statue, long after the dialling tone had become the only sound from the instrument clutched in her hand.

Georgina had never been more grateful for her thriving little business in the period after her break with Janus. Once it seemed quite definite she would never see him again she achieved a strange kind of fatalistic serenity, which, although it lent a new touch of artistry to some of the exquisite floral confections she created, quite failed to stop her losing weight, despite all efforts to remedy this by her mother at weekends or Chris and Karen with their goodies during the week. Georgina's clothes began to hang loose on her, and there were shadows beneath the eyes which these days rarely displayed their old, familiar sparkle.

All three employees of Castle Florists were enjoying a much deserved tea-break one Sunday afternoon when Chris answered the telephone and immediately passed it over to Georgina.

'Someone called Katherine Harvey, love,' she whispered.

Mystified, Georgina took the receiver to discover her caller was Janus's sister, Katie, who sounded very worried as she explained her grandmother was asking for Georgina, and was it at all possible for Georgina to come to Keyne Magna, preferably pretty quickly.

'Oh, my goodness,' said Georgina in alarm. 'Is she terribly ill?'

'She's very low. It's her heart, as you know, Georgina. And Dad's in the States with Miles, Janus is in Holland somewhere, and I haven't been able to contact any of them yet. Not that it matters. She's adamant it's you she wants to see. She—she says there's something she must say to you before it's too late. So could you come—please?'

'Oh, no! I mean, yes—of course,' said Georgina, horrified. 'Don't worry. I'll be with you as soon as I can. How about Rosalind?'

'Away, worse luck. But in any case it's you Gran wants, not Ros.'

'Right—I'll be on my way in a few minutes.'

Georgina left the shop for Chris to lock up, rang her mother to say she wouldn't be home for the weekend, then threw some things into an overnight bag and ran for her Mini, thankful to see the petrol tank was full as she made for the M4. The journey to Wiltshire seemed endless. Georgina, desperately worried Mrs Stanhope might actually die before she got there, pushed her ancient little car as hard as she could, but it was later than she would have liked when she finally arrived in Keyne Magna, tense and strung-up at the prospect of what might await her at Glebe House.

Katie, her fair, pretty face strained, came running out to meet Georgina the moment the car came to a halt.

'Thank goodness you're here—I was getting worried.'

'Sorry to take so long. How's Mrs Stanhope?'

Katie took Georgina by the hand and led her into the house. 'Come and see her. She sleeps on the ground floor, as you probably know. It's years since we've let her climb stairs.'

'Is she very ill?' asked Georgina fearfully, hanging back a little as Katie went ahead of her down the hall to the separate suite of rooms on the far side of the house.

'She's holding her own,' said Katie non-committally, and opened the door quietly into a darkened room with its curtains drawn against the fading light. Mrs Stanhope lay like an effigy, her face in shadow, her hands folded on top of the counterpane. It was impossible to tell whether the old lady was still breathing.

Georgina gazed at her fearfully, then tensed as a tall figure rose from beside the bed.

'You remember Angus?' whispered Katie.

Georgina, certain for a moment it had been Janus, felt sick with disappointment.

'Nice of you to come,' whispered Katie's young husband. 'Would you sit with her for a while? She's sleeping.'

'Yes, of course,' Georgina whispered back, hoping she sounded less scared than she felt.

'Just for a few minutes,' said Katie. 'I'll make some coffee. Would you like something to eat?'

Georgina shook her head blindly. The mere idea of food seemed like sacrilege.

The others slid silently from the room, leaving Georgina to tiptoe to the chair placed a little way from the bed. She sat gingerly, her heart beating so loudly she was sure it must be audible in the quiet room. Henrietta Stanhope lay with her head turned away, looking fragile and defenceless without the indomitable quality she exuded when awake. Georgina tried to relax. She sat back in the chair, feeling suddenly very frightened and young, shaken by unbearable longing for Janus now she was here in his family home. Life had begun to seem possible without him in her own familiar surroundings, but here it was not. She bit her lip hard, staring down at her clasped hands as she fought against the tears she'd refused to shed ever since his last phone call. Now the dam of her self-control threatened to give way at the sight of the still figure in the bed. It took superhuman effort not to bury her head in her hands and cry her eyes out.

'Georgina?' The reed-like whisper brought Georgina's heart to her throat as she realised Mrs Stanhope was awake. She started to her feet, but a transparent, veined hand waved her back. 'No, child. Sit down. I get nervous when people hang over me.'

Georgina smiled despite her distress. The flesh might be feeble, but the spirit was still alive and kicking. 'How are you, Mrs Stanhope?'

'As you see, my dear.' She gave a ghost of a chuckle. 'Now tell me how you are.'

'Fine,' said Georgina brightly. 'Busy, of course. Lots of weddings this time of year.'

'And funerals all year round!' There was so wicked a gleam in the sunken eyes that Georgina could only grin back.

'Afraid so.'

'Good girl. Not afraid to face facts.'

Georgina cleared her throat valiantly. 'I'd rather not talk about funerals, just the same, Mrs Stanhope. You've got more bottle than me.'

'If I thought that I wouldn't have asked you to come.' As the old lady gave a dry little cough Georgina flew out of her seat, prepared to give whatever assistance was necessary, but Mrs Stanhope waved her back again. 'Stay where you are, child. I'm not on my way out just yet.'

Deeply relieved to hear it, Georgina relaxed a little, feeling better now it seemed Mrs Stanhope wasn't about to fade out of life before her very eyes.

'Are you perfectly happy, Georgina?' went on the old lady, surprising her.

Georgina hesitated, tempted to say few people were perfectly happy, but Henrietta Stanhope's death-bed seemed no place for evasion. 'No,' she said baldly. 'I'm not.'

There was silence for a moment, as though the invalid was thinking this over.

'Janus is unhappy, too,' she said after a while.

Georgina's nails bit into the palms of her hands. 'I'm sorry to hear that.'

'Are you? Yet you're the one making him unhappy.'

Georgina stared, speechless, at the still figure in the bed. How much did Mrs Stanhope know? Or did people nearing their end develop extra powers of discernment?

'Do you love him, child?'

What was the point in denying it, thought Georgina. 'Yes, Mrs Stanhope. I do.'

'I thought so. He loves you too, you know.'

'No, I don't.'

'Nonsense, child. Women always know.'

Georgina sniffed inelegantly. 'I—I knew he fancied me, of course.'

'*Fancied?* Say what you mean, girl. He wanted to make love to you, I suppose.'

Georgina nodded. 'I almost let him, too, but right at the last minute I couldn't go through with it.'

'Why? Isn't he any good as a lover?'

Heat surged in Georgina's face as she stared down at her clasped hands. This was nothing like her idea of a death-bed conversation, yet to her surprise she felt no embarrassment in admitting that Janus was all the lover she'd ever dreamed about. 'But it all happened in a rush. Sort of by accident. I didn't want my first time to be like that, if only on principle,' she added candidly.

There was a silent wheezing from the bed which frightened Georgina out of her wits until she realised it was Mrs Stanhope's laughter.

'You booted him out of your bed because of your principles?'

'Well—yes.'

'Principles are poor substitutes for a strong, warm body to hold you close at night, girl.'

Georgina's eyes opened wide in shock, and the wheeze of laughter strengthened.

'I wasn't always old and infirm, Miss!'

'I'm sure you left a trail of broken hearts all over the place in your time, Mrs Stanhope.'

'Pooh! Not all that many.' Mrs Stanhope paused for breath. 'But in my day, y'see, you couldn't hop in and out of bed with chaps. You had to make certain you'd found the right one—and married him—before there was any hanky-panky.'

Georgina chuckled. 'My sentiments exactly. I've been waiting to make sure of the same thing. That's what I meant by principles.'

Mrs Stanhope gave a faint, gleeful cackle, much to Katie's astonishment as she came in to say time was up and Georgina must have something to drink, even if she wouldn't eat.

'Off your food?' asked the old lady in a flash.

'A bit.'

'Thought you looked a bit peaky.'

'She rushed here straight from her shop,' said Katie. 'So you have a rest, Gran. I'll send Georgina back later after she's had a meal and maybe a bath if she wants.'

Now the initial ordeal was over, and Georgina felt rather happier about Mrs Stanhope's immediate prospects, she found she was more in the mood for food than for some time. The new bride, rather proud of her cooking, had prepared a freshly baked salmon flan and a tempting salad for the weary guest.

'We've eaten,' she said, as she pulled out a chair for Georgina. 'Angus will sit with Gran for a while, so relax. You looked like a ghost when you go here.'

'I'm not surprised! I was terrified of what I might find.'

Katie sat down opposite, eyeing Georgina thoughtfully. 'We've only met twice before, of course, but I fancy you've lost a lot of weight since I saw you last.' She poured coffee for herself. 'By the way, please don't worry about all that nonsense Miles involved you in—pretending to be his fiancée and all that.'

Georgina pulled a face as she began to eat. 'You must think I'm an idiot.'

'No. That's Miles's role.' Katie scowled. 'What a moron he can be when he likes.'

'I'll steer very clear of his schemes in future.' Georgina looked squarely into Katie's blue eyes. 'The thing I regret most is having hurt Rosalind, however unintentionally. I like her very much.'

'She likes you, Georgina.' Katie hesitated. 'She likes Harry, too, you know.'

'Good. Harry, I assure you, is most definitely *not* an idiot. She won't come to any grief with him.' Georgina put down her fork after only a few mouthfuls, glad of the cup of coffee Katie pushed towards her. 'Tell me. How bad *is* your grandmother?'

Katie's eyes fell. 'There's nothing can be done, if that's what you mean. The doctor says to keep up with the medication, humour her, see she's kept happy, that she could go any minute—or not, as the case may be.'

'How about your father and Miles—and Janus? Shouldn't they be home?'

'Dad and Miles arrive back tomorrow. I'm not precisely sure about Janus.' Katie smiled reassuringly. 'But don't worry. Now she's got her way and seen you she'll probably rally for a bit. What did she want, by the way?'

Georgina frowned. 'I've no idea. She didn't say.'

Katie shook her head indulgently. 'She's a canny old bird, our Henrietta. Likes to play her cards close to her chest. She must have some bee in her bonnet, the old darling, but it's not a blind bit of use asking what it is until she's ready to let us know.'

'Shall I go back to her now?'

'Want a bath first?'

'Yes, please,' said Georgina fervently. 'I'm still in my working gear. I'd sell my soul for hot water and a change of clothes.'

Katie got up briskly. 'Come on, then.' She smiled at Georgina. 'I'm glad you came. I've been dying to see you again because Gran says Janus is crazy about you.'

Georgina bit her lip, startled. 'If he is he's got a funny way of showing it.'

Katie hoisted Georgina's bag and led her across the hall to the stairs. She grinned over her shoulder. 'There's certainly something horribly wrong with his world at the moment. I think Gran may well be right. And *I* may be wrong, of course, but from the look of you I rather fancy you feel the same way about him!' She ushered a dazed Georgina into a different room from the one she'd slept in before. 'I'll go down to Gran now. Join us when you're ready.'

The rest of the evening was a blur to Georgina. She spent much of it watching television with Katie or Angus, and every so often took her turn to sit for a few minutes with Mrs Stanhope, who dozed most of the time, her breathing moving the coverlet so little that Georgina sat in a permanent state of tension as she waited in vain to learn the reason for her summons to Mrs Stanhope's bedside.

At ten Katie sent an exhausted Georgina to bed. Her grandmother, she said firmly, was given some pills at this stage, after which she usually slept until morning. And even if the worst came to the worst and Georgina's presence was required during the night Katie promised she would come and fetch her.

Georgina thanked her, asked to make a phone call, then bade Angus and Katie goodnight. After a brief, reassuring word to her mother she prepared for bed in the unfamiliar room, too tired to do anything but brush her teeth before sliding into bed. In spite of the strange room and the tensions of the day she fell asleep fairly quickly, but began to dream instantly, formless, fragmented dreams which merged one into another until a dream more vivid and real superseded the rest. She was running, running, trying to catch up with Janus, who strode ahead of her without a backward glance, ignoring her efforts to reach him. Tears poured down her face, she stretched out her arms imploringly, and at last he turned to catch her close, and they were together, clasping each other so strongly she could smell the fragrance of his skin, feel the warmth of it . . . She woke with a stifled cry on her lips as she found her dream was no dream at all. She was held tightly against a familiar bare chest and Janus was staring down at her as though he couldn't believe his eyes, his face as pale as hers in the moonlight streaming into the shadowy bedroom.

CHAPTER NINE

'YOU were dreaming,' Janus said, and tightened his hold as Georgina, fully awake by this time, tried to scramble away. 'I think I must be too! How the hell do you come to be in my bed?'

Georgina stared at him wide-eyed. 'I didn't know it was your bed.'

'I can well believe that!' Janus released her, then sat down on the edge of the bed. Georgina dragged the coverlet up to her chin and peered at him owlishly, recovered enough to see, with relief, that although his shirt was missing, draped, she could see, over a chair in the corner, Janus seemed otherwise decently covered.

'Your grandmother!' she gasped, with sudden, shocking recall of just why she was here in his room. 'Is she worse?'

He looked blank. 'Worse?'

'That's why I'm here.'

'In my bed?'

'In your house! Your grandmother sent for me. There was something she wanted to tell me before——' Georgina gulped, trying to find some way of breaking it to him gently. 'Before it was too late.'

Janus looked startled. 'What do you mean, too late? She's sleeping peacefully at the moment.'

Georgina flopped back against the pillow, limp with relief. 'Thank goodness—I thought...'

Janus was quite plainly having problems in coping with so many shocks at once. 'What was this urgent something she had to tell you?' he demanded.

'I don't know. She hasn't actually told me yet.'

'Extraordinary!' He looked about him, thrusting a hand through his hair. 'I quite obviously shouldn't be here—I'd better go.'

'When did you arrive?'

'A few minutes ago. No one saw fit to let me know they'd sub-let my room.'

'I suppose Katie's in bed.'

'Yes. She is.'

There was a tense pause. Georgina smiled uncertainly at him. 'I'm sorry to turn you out.'

'Why were you crying?' he asked abruptly.

'Crying?'

'The moon was so bright I didn't bother with a light when I came in here. I didn't realise my bed was occupied until you started to cry.'

Georgina huddled lower under the covers. 'I was dreaming,' she muttered.

'A nightmare, by the sound of it.'

'No. It wasn't a nightmare.' In fact, she thought, it was a dream come true once he'd taken her in his arms.

'Georgina...' He moved nearer the bed, into the moonlight which fell full on his scarred face, showing up sharper angles and hollows than she remembered. A sudden flood of love and longing swept over Georgina as she gazed up at him, willing him to go on.

'Yes?' she prompted very softly.

He smiled, one side of his mouth tilting towards the scar, and she swallowed hard at the sight of it.

'You've said what I wanted to hear!' He put one knee on the bed, balancing on his outstretched hands as he leaned towards her.

'What *did* I say?'

'You said "yes",' he whispered and kissed her gently.

Georgina trembled at the touch of his mouth, but drew back, her hair tumbling over her shoulders as her eyes met his. 'We seem to have taken a short cut somehow since we last met. You said there was too wide a gap between us, remember!'

'I believe I know a way to bridge it.' Janus sat down on the bed and swung his legs up. With a casual air he propped pillows against the carved headboard, then startled Georgina by taking her by the elbows and pulling her on to his lap as he leaned back with a sigh, cradling her against his chest.

'I've given a lot of thought to the subject since our last unhappy exchange on the telephone, Georgina, and I've come to the conclusion that I don't care a hang about any so-called differences between us, or anything at all other than the fact that I'm bloody miserable without you. Are you miserable too?' He shook her gently. 'Say something, little one!'

Georgina, for a variety of reasons, found it utterly impossible to say anything. The mere fact of being alone with Janus in a darkened bedroom in the middle of the night, held close in his arms, prevented her brain from functioning at all.

'Cat got your tongue?' he asked, laughing under his breath, and put a hand under her chin, brought her mouth to his and proceeded to discover for himself that her tongue was exactly where it should be, responding helplessly to his as he kissed her in a way which put an end to any further conversation.

It was a long, long time before Georgina recovered her senses sufficiently to push him away a little. 'We shouldn't be doing this!' she said guiltily.

'Why not?' Janus began kissing her again, his hands investigating every line and curve of the body pressed to his. 'My grandmother would approve,' he assured her unsteadily at one point. 'You have my word on that.'

Georgina giggled. 'I know. She told me principles made poor bedfellows.'

Janus shook with laughter against her, his urgency suddenly lessened as he smoothed Georgina's hair away from her face. 'Do you think that was what she wanted to tell you?'

'Janus!' Georgina slid out of his arms to sit crosslegged on the bed beside him. 'How can you joke about it?'

'Because at this moment I feel I could joke about anything,' he assured her. 'I have not been in a joking mood lately—not since the occasion of Harry's party, to be precise. Seeing you that night, laughing and dancing with Miles's mates, made me so damn jealous I wanted to throw you over my shoulder and haul you out of there. I could have murdered you.'

'Really?' she said, starry-eyed.

Janus reached to turn on the bedside lamp, then leaned against the headboard, his eyes travelling from Georgina's bare toes, up over her striped cotton pyjamas to the fiery mass of dishevelled hair, coming to rest on her suddenly self-conscious face. He smiled slowly, his eyes dancing above smudges of fatigue which matched her own.

'Do you always wear men's pyjamas to bed?'

'No. I keep these for visiting. Normally I sleep *au naturel*.' Georgina pulled a face. 'Good thing I didn't tonight, isn't it?'

Janus cast his eyes piously heavenwards. 'A very good thing. If you had I rather fancy all hell would have broken loose when I found you crying into my pillow.' He frowned. 'You look a bit under par, little one. Have you been ill?'

'No, just excessively depressed and miserable.'

They gazed at each other in silence.

'If,' began Janus with great care, 'you were miserable over my absence, is it possible you are happy about my presence? Like right now?'

'Oh, I am, I am!'

He nodded approvingly. 'Good. I'm happy about yours, too, euphoric even. In fact I'm still recovering from the miracle of finding you in my bed.'

'Katie put me in here.'

'Did she, now?' His eyes narrowed, then he smiled. 'I'm exceedingly grateful to my little sister, but I can't help wondering . . . No matter. To return to what I was saying. I've got a birthday next Tuesday——'

Georgina's crow of delight interrupted him. 'You're never going to believe this—so have I!' She smiled all over her face. 'I'm twenty-one on the same day. We've got a birthday in common, Janus.'

'Oh, my darling,' he breathed, sitting upright. 'That's not all we have in common.' He put out his hands and Georgina put hers into them, leaning forward to put her lips against his, and he dropped her hands and pulled her into his arms and kissed her until their hearts were hammering.

'You're a witch,' he said against her lips. 'With you in my arms I can forget everything except that I just want to go on doing this forever.'

'Oh, yes, please!' she breathed fervently, and wriggled closer, delighting in his sharp intake of breath.

'But,' he said unsteadily, putting her away slightly, 'the nature of the beast being what it is I shan't be able to go on kissing you without wanting to do a great deal more than that, so I'm getting out of here fast.'

And, ignoring all her protestations, he thrust her under the covers, bent and kissed her swiftly on her parted lips and switched off the light.

'Goodnight, darling,' he said caressingly from the door. 'I'll see you in the morning.'

'Goodnight—but I won't be able to sleep,' she said, sighing.

'Neither shall I. I told you we had a lot in common!'

Georgina dozed and dreamed and woke to find the moonlight gone and the sky just beginning to pale as the door opened very quietly and Janus whispered, 'Are you awake?'

Her heart thumped. 'Yes.'

He came in with a tray, put it down beside Georgina, then went back to close the door.

'Your grandmother?' she asked urgently.

'That's why I'm here,' he reassured her. 'She's fine. Remarkably so, in fact.'

'Really?' Georgina smiled radiantly. 'Oh, Janus, that's wonderful.'

Janus sat down beside her, yawning a little, his long brown legs bare below his white towelling dressing gown. 'I thought you might like some tea.'

'I'd love some tea,' she said happily. 'In fact I love everything and everyone in the world at this particular moment. Where did you sleep?'

'In my father's room. But I didn't sleep much. Did you?'

'No.'

They gazed at each other in silence.

'Shall I pour?' asked Georgina at last.

'Please.'

She smiled. 'I don't even know how you like your tea.'

'Strong, with a dash of milk.'

'Do you really? So do I.'

He nodded smugly. 'You see? Perfectly suited, give or take a few years.'

'You're as old as you feel,' Georgina said firmly.

'Which is like a schoolboy, and a lovesick one at that when you look at me the way you're doing right this minute!' Janus touched a finger to the tip of her nose. 'Actually, I took a chance on waking you up because I couldn't wait to tell you something very, very interesting.'

'What is it?'

Janus, it seemed, had been so disinclined for sleep he'd decided to take a walk in the garden half an hour earlier. 'I didn't want to chance waking Gran by going into her bedroom, so I took a look through her small side window as I passed by, just to make sure she was all right. Imagine my surprise, little one, when I found every light in her room blazing, and there, propped up in bed with a large-print thriller, actually smoking a cigarette, would you believe, was darling Henrietta, looking no more moribund than you or me.'

Georgina's eyes opened like saucers. 'You mean she's taken a turn for the better?'

'Always supposing she was ill in the first place!' Janus grinned. 'I rather think she's been having us on.'

Georgina frowned incredulously. 'But why on earth would she frighten her family like that?'

'Not the family. Just you—and me. I rather think it was a ploy to bring us together, unless I'm very much mistaken!' Janus's smile was crooked. 'You remember the lady I mentioned—the one I ran to for consolation?'

Georgina stared at him, her eyes flying storm signals. 'You meant your *grandmother* all the time?'

'Yes, ma'am.'

'And you let me think you were dashing off to Liza Verreker or someone?'

'How did I know you'd care?'

'You must have known!'

'Not until now.'

Her eyes fell before the caressing look in his. 'So just exactly what did you tell Mrs Stanhope?'

'That I'd fallen hopelessly in love with you, but one way and another I'd made a complete hash of things and felt miserable as sin.' Janus smiled impenitently. 'So she decided to stage a little drama, I think, to bring us together. Katie would have been all agog to help, of course. Just up her street. Now she's married she thinks everyone else should be, too. Besides, it was very easy for our Henrietta. She really does have a weak heart, you see, darling, and uses it shamelessly to get her own way. We never know whether she's crying wolf or not, so none of us ever cares to take any chances. Which,' he added, suddenly sober, 'is how I was lucky enough to meet you. If Miles hadn't been scared of upsetting Gran with his Linda Potts I might never have met you again.'

Georgina took some time to digest all this. 'Does this mean she approves of me?' she asked diffidently. 'For you, I mean?'

'She certainly wouldn't have gone to all this trouble otherwise,' he assured her. 'Not, I'll admit, that it would have been much trouble. She's probably been enjoying herself no end.' He touched Georgina's hand. 'Don't be cross with her. She just wants me to be happy.'

'I'm not in the least cross with her, because I just want you to be happy, too,' said Georgina, deciding the time for pretence of any kind was over.

Janus looked hard at her. She smiled. He took the cup from her hand and replaced it with his own on the tray, then leaned forward and kissed her mouth.

'Shall I tell you how very easy it is to make me happy?' he whispered.

'Yes.'

'That's it. You're getting the idea. All you have to do is answer in the affirmative to the following questions, Miss Griffiths. Is that clear?'

'Yes.'

'Good. Question one. Do you love me?'

'Yes.'

His eyes blazed in triumph. 'Then you'll marry me?'

'Yes.'

'Soon?'

'Yes, yes, yes!'

'Full marks!' Janus caught her in his arms and rocked her back and forth, laughing softly as he planted kisses all over her radiant face. 'I told you I'd kiss every freckle one day.'

'Why not start on the rest right now?'

He sat very still, looking down into her eyes. 'That's fighting talk, Georgina.'

'Just a statement of fact.'

He sighed raggedly. 'I'd better go.'

'Stay. Please. It's too early to get up.'

'You didn't say stay last night.'

'Last night I thought your grandmother was dying. Now I know she isn't I want to celebrate life in the best possible way. Make love to me, Janus.'

He looked deep into her eyes. 'There's nothing I want more. I've wanted you near me like this every minute of every day since I last saw you. But one advantage of experience is that I know there's a lot more to marriage than bed. I've found plenty of women I liked sharing a bed with—and don't you dare try to kick me again, you termagant!'

'I hate the thought of those other women,' she said fiercely.

'Let me finish. What I intended to say was that I've never met anyone I wanted to share my *life* with before.'

Georgina melted against him. 'Oh, Janus, what a wonderful thing to say. I never have, either.'

'You've hardly had time to find out.'

'Will you give me some?'

'No bloody fear!' And Janus forgot about his principles and his grandmother and everything else in the world as he slid beneath the covers to take her in his arms.

Georgina, imagining his intent was to make love to her there and then, relaxed as he cradled her against him with her head on his shoulder.

'No,' he said softly, 'I refuse to pounce on you forthwith just because you've agreed to marry me.' He yawned. 'It's very early, I've had no sleep worth mentioning, and I'll be perfectly happy just to lie here for a few minutes with you in my arms—just to break you in to the idea of sharing a bed with me till death do us part. It might be a good idea to know what you're letting yourself in for.'

'Oh. I see.' Georgina snuggled against him with a sigh. 'Why? Do you snore?'

'I've had no complaints so far—ouch! Don't be so violent, you bully!'

'Then stop referring—even obliquely—to former encounters with members of my sex.' Georgina heaved herself up to frown at him with mock severity. 'For one thing it isn't fair. You know I haven't had any. Not the physical kind.'

Janus looked up at her with an odd expression in his eyes. 'I do know. I also know I frightened you to death on the one never-to-be-forgotten occasion when I lost my head sufficiently to try to make love to you.'

'It wasn't fright that made me put a stop to things,' she informed him matter of factly.

'Then what the hell was it?'

Georgina lay down, curling against him with her head on his shoulder. 'Your grandmother and I have a lot in common. She said in her day one had to settle on one's man and marry him before there was any—well, hanky-panky is how she put it.'

Janus jerked her face up to his. 'Good grief, just what have you two been talking about altogether?'

'You, mainly.'

His eyes bored into hers. 'You still haven't told me why you pushed me away that night.'

'You hadn't said you loved me, or even that you had any intention of making the occasion more than just a one-off,' said Georgina apologetically.

'Oh, I see. You thought I'd say thank you politely once we'd made love and vanish into the blue!'

Georgina reached up both hands either side of his scowling face and brought it down to hers so she could kiss him. 'Not exactly,' she said soothingly. 'It was just that I knew perfectly well that if you did make love to me it would spoil me for any other man. So, heaven knows how, I found the strength to push you away—and alienated you pretty comprehensively while I was at it.'

Janus looked very stern in the pale dawn light. 'Our lines of communication managed to get pretty snarled, didn't they?' He pulled her close, kissing her fiercely. 'In case you're still in any doubt, madam, *you've* spoilt *me* for any other woman since I first set eyes on you. Why do you think I look so damn haggard? You're the first woman I've ever lost any sleep over in my entire life.'

Georgina slid her arms round him. 'Then put your head on my shoulder and go to sleep for a bit now.'

There was silence for a while.

'Darling,' said Janus in a constricted voice, 'at this moment I'm not tired at all. Quite the reverse. I'd better go.'

Georgina tilted her head back, smiling at him. 'Stay. Please.'

Janus stared down at her for the space of a heartbeat, a pulse beating alongside his mouth. 'Are you frightened now?' he whispered.

She shook her head, her eyes alight with such unmistakable invitation that he said no more about leaving, or about anything else at all except to whisper how much he loved and wanted her as he proceeded, with infinite care and sensitivity, to awaken her to the full response her body was capable of in answer to his. His lips moved over her lovingly, lingering in certain sensitive places as he achieved his ambition of kissing every freckle she possessed, and Georgina trembled beneath his caresses, moved to make tentative caresses of her own in response as all the misery of the past few weeks melted away as if it had never been. Her eyes glittered with the joy of each new discovery as, with mounting heat, Janus led her step by step towards the moment when he had no choice but to hurt her for a fleeting moment, and Georgina gasped against his urgent mouth, her eyes dilating for an instant before they opened wide to stare into his in triumph as she found her body knew exactly how to join with his to achieve the rapture she had known from the beginning she would find in loving Janus.

Pale early sunshine was streaming into the room before Janus could bring himself to leave it.

'Darling, I must go.'

Georgina's arms tightened round him. 'We never drank the tea after all.'

Janus buried his face in her dishevelled curls. 'No. We didn't.'

'I'll go down and make some more,' she said, detaching herself.

'Could you possibly cook something, too?' he asked, grinning all over his face like a schoolboy. 'I never got any dinner last night. I'm starving.'

Georgina slid out of bed, resuming her pyjama jacket hurriedly, something in the way his bright, narrowed eyes were watching her fingers as she did it up telling her that given the slightest encouragement Janus might pull her back into bed.

'Get dressed and leave me to do likewise,' she said, trying hard to be brisk, 'and I'll cook whatever you like. Only I think I'd better pop in and have a look at your grandmother first.'

Janus grinned as he shrugged himself into his dressing-gown. 'Ah, yes! You go first and I'll join you in her room as soon as I've got rid of this stubble. I'm rather looking forward to the confrontation!' He came round the bed to take Georgina in his arms. 'Well, little one? Do you still want to marry me?'

'Yes, please.' She buried her face against his shoulder. 'But not just because we've made love, Janus.'

'I hope, my darling, that you're marrying me because you love me,' he said severely. 'Do you?'

She nodded vigorously. 'Yes.'

'Good. I love you, too. But I've already told you that, over and over, only a very short while ago.'

'That could have been just the heat of the moment!'

'It could. But it wasn't. I've never actually said those three little words to anyone before in my life, Georgina Griffiths.' He kissed her lingeringly, and she melted against him in immediate response, and it was several minutes before Janus finally went quietly from the room to leave her to dress.

Georgina was amazed that it was still only eight in the morning by the time she arrived in the Stanhope kitchen. She felt as though she'd lived through a whole lifetime since her arrival the previous evening. The house was very quiet as she washed up their teacups and restored them to their places on the huge pine dresser which filled one wall of the kitchen, and, since there was no sign of Katie and Angus, she went quietly along the hall leading to Mrs Stanhope's room, and knocked on the door.

There was a slight scuffle within, then a faint voice said 'come in'. Georgina, her fact suitably composed into grave enquiry, opened the door and crossed the room towards the bed. The curtains were drawn against the morning light, and Henrietta Stanhope lay, as before, very still against her pillows, her hands folded on the covers, her face in the shadows.

'Good morning, Mrs Stanhope. How are you today?'

One of the hands lifted slightly. 'As you see, my dear,' sighed the invalid.

'Can I fetch you anything?'

'No, no. Katie will be down soon. She knows what I have.'

'I'll just sit with you for a while, then, shall I?' offered Georgina.

Mrs Stanhope nodded meekly. 'If you like, child.'

Georgina took the same chair as the evening before, still placed a fair distance from the bed, so that it was hard to see the invalid's face very clearly in the underwater gloom created by the heavy green silk curtains. As she sat down Janus came in, dressed in a grey tracksuit, his damp hair curling tightly after a shower. He moved round the bed and took one of his grandmother's hands in his.

'I've heard the news, Gran,' he said, a catch in his voice. 'But you just hold on—I know Dad and Miles will get back as quickly as they can, and Katie told me you'd asked Georgina to come. Good morning, Georgina,' he added gravely.

'Good morning,' responded Georgina in kind, swallowing on the giggle threatening to vanquish her.

'I'm not dead yet,' said Mrs Stanhope, her voice much less reedy. Her dark eyes looked up into his languishingly. 'I hope you don't mind meeting Georgina like this, dear boy.'

'Not in the least,' Janus said cheerfully, and threw back the curtains. 'Let's have some light, shall we?'

'No!' cried Mrs Stanhope, putting her hands over her eyes. 'I can't bear the light.'

Janus held out a hand to Georgina, who ran to him, leaning against him as he slid his arm round her waist. 'Open your eyes, Henrietta Stanhope,' he commanded.

Something in his voice made the sharp old eyes peer through the lattice of her fingers, then Mrs Stanhope dropped her hands and struggled upright. Georgina flew to stack pillows behind her, her eyes narrowing suspiciously as she saw the thick layer of white powder on the old lady's face.

'I know, I know,' said Mrs Stanhope impatiently. 'But someone had to do something! I told Katie you were behaving like a silly schoolboy over young Georgina here, Janus. So we concocted a little plan.' She eyed her grandson with a smugness justified by the fact that he pulled the chair nearer the bed and sat Georgina down on his lap, cuddling her openly. 'From here, it looks as though it worked!'

'But, Mrs Stanhope, you frightened the life out of me!' scolded Georgina. 'When Katie rang up to say you were dying——'

'She told me she avoided any mention of actual demise,' contradicted Mrs Stanhope. 'I gave her strict instructions to say I was very low.'

Georgina thought hard. 'Well, yes, I suppose she did.'

'That was no lie. I *was* low. And all because Janus here was low too—positively in the depths over you, child.' A fiendish grin lit the shrewd eyes. 'And when you arrived, all eyes and freckles and visibly thinner than when I saw you last, I knew I'd done the right thing. *You* were eating your heart out too, or my name's not Henrietta.'

'It should be Machiavelli,' retorted Janus, then stood Georgina on her feet, eyeing her up and down. Her black cotton sweater and cream linen trousers were new, and a size smaller than any adult clothes she'd owned before. 'Whereas you, little one, can no longer object to the description.' His eyes met hers significantly. 'I never even noticed how much weight you've lost.'

She smiled at him and resumed her place on his knee. 'Like a proper Victorian miss,' she agreed happily. 'You sent me into a decline.'

'Do I take it,' enquired Mrs Stanhope, 'that all is now settled between you?'

Janus nodded absently, still gazing down into Georgina's face. 'More or less.'

'How about your shop, my dear?'

'My partner will be only too happy to buy me out, I think. Then Janus has promised to buy me a share in a business somewhere near enough to London for him to commute.'

Mrs Stanhope eyed them with interest. 'How have you managed to settle so much when it's still not even breakfast-time?'

'Katie forgot to tell me she'd put Georgina in my room,' said Janus, to the latter's horror.

'Oh, that was my idea,' said Mrs Stanhope airily. 'As I said to Georgina last night, there's no real substitute for two bodies in a bed together. You're no grandson of mine if you didn't take full advantage of the situation.'

'You,' said Janus, grinning, 'are a very wicked old woman. And I love you.' And, pulling Georgina to her feet with him, he bent to kiss his grandmother.

'Me too,' said Georgina, doing likewise.

There was a brightness in the old eyes for a moment, then Mrs Stanhope pushed them away. 'Then for heaven's sake get out of here so I can get up out of this boring bed, and wash this filthy stuff off my face! Janus, you get Katie and Angus up, and could you be a love, Georgina, and make a start on some breakfast? Madge is on holiday. By the way, do you think your mother might like the marquee we had for Katie's wedding? And you will invite Rosalind, won't you, because I fancy she's set her sights on that brother of yours, Georgina. Serves Miles right. And don't wear white, child. One of those ivory tints would do better with your colouring——'

Convulsed with laughter, Janus pulled Georgina from the room and took her in his arms. 'Are you sure you want to marry into a family like mine?'

'You haven't met any of mine yet—except Harry.'

'Ah, yes. Harry. He was distinctly cool towards me the night of his party.'

Georgina nodded blithely. 'He was afraid I'd get hurt if I hankered after you.'

Janus sobered. 'Will he come round if I promise that I'll take damn good care you never get hurt again—by me or anyone else?'

'I should think so.' She met his eyes very squarely. 'But, fond of him though I am, it wouldn't make any difference if Harry did disapprove. I may be relatively young, but I know perfectly well that you're the only man I could ever love, Janus, which is all that matters to me.'

He shook his head slowly, his eyes filled with a light which made her tremble. 'What did I ever do to deserve you, little one?' He kissed her lingeringly, then slid his arm round her waist to walk very slowly towards the hall, pausing to kiss her again before they separated to do Mrs Stanhope's bidding. The kiss lengthened, their absorption in each other so absolute that they failed to notice the infuriated young man standing in the open doorway glaring at them.

'Janus!' roared Miles Stanhope, incensed. 'What the hell do you think you're playing at?'

'Why, hello, Miles, welcome home.' Janus raised his head with a grin, keeping Georgina close in his arms. 'Since you ask, I'm not playing at anything. I've never been more serious in my life, which is why I was kissing Georgina.'

Miles glared at him. 'That much I could see for myself. What beats me is why you're doing it in Glebe House at this hour of the morning!'

'Because your congratulations are in order, old son. Georgina is now *my* fiancée, and there's no play-acting about this engagement, believe me.' Janus released his future bride to clap his brother on the shoulder. 'Not that I won't be eternally grateful for the role you played in bringing Georgina and me together, believe me.'

Miles put down his suitcase with a thump. 'The role being Bobo the clown, you mean, where women are concerned!' He stared at them bitterly. 'Linda's moved in with a journalist from the rag which published that damn photograph. Ros is wining and dining every five minutes with Harry Rawlings, the chap I used to call friend. And now you, Gee. You're by way of being the last straw!'

Georgina exchanged a laughing glance with Janus, then planted a kiss on his brother's glum face. 'Cheer up, love. You haven't lost out completely. You've gained a sister-in-law instead of a fiancée, that's all.' She gave him an affectionate hug. 'And you were way off the mark about the clown bit—the role you played to perfection, Miles, was Cupid!'

MY VALENTINE 1992

Celebrate the most romantic day of the year with
MY VALENTINE 1992—a sexy new collection of four
romantic stories written by our famous Temptation
authors:

> GINA WILKINS
> KRISTINE ROLOFSON
> JOANN ROSS
> VICKI LEWIS THOMPSON

My Valentine 1992—an exquisite escape into a romantic
and sensuous world.

 Harlequin Books

VAL-92-R

HARLEQUIN
PROUDLY PRESENTS
A DAZZLING NEW CONCEPT IN ROMANCE FICTION

One small town—twelve terrific love stories

Welcome to Tyler, Wisconsin—a town full of people
you'll enjoy getting to know, memorable friends and
unforgettable lovers, and a long-buried secret that
lurks beneath its serene surface....

JOIN US FOR A YEAR IN THE LIFE OF TYLER

Each book set in Tyler is a self-contained love story;
together, the twelve novels stitch the fabric of a
community.

LOSE YOUR HEART TO TYLER!

The excitement begins in March 1992, with
WHIRLWIND, by Nancy Martin. When lively, brash
Liza Baron arrives home unexpectedly, she moves
into the old family lodge, where the silent and
mysterious Cliff Forrester has been living in seclusion
for years....

WATCH FOR ALL TWELVE BOOKS
OF THE TYLER SERIES
Available wherever Harlequin books are sold